Everyday
Black People
In Strange Situations

Evan Ross Burton

**HOT SECOND
BOOKS**

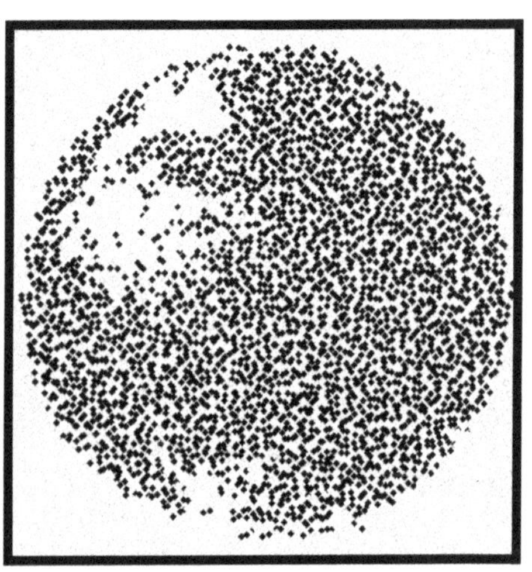

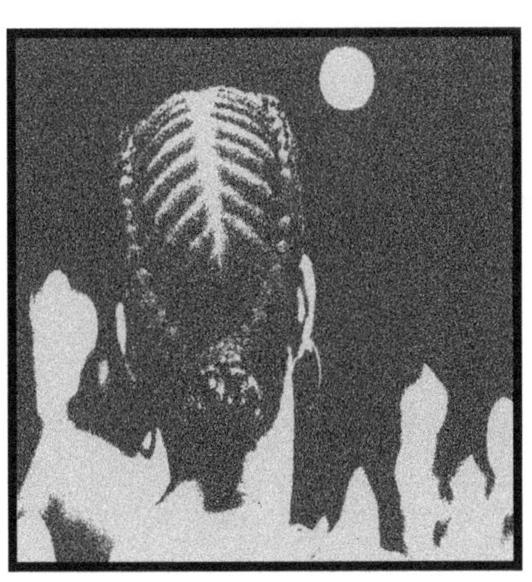

ISBN: 979-8-218-69662-7

EVERYDAY BLACK PEOPLE IN STRANGE SITUATIONS

*With love for you and us
and future generations.*

EVERYDAY BLACK PEOPLE IN STRANGE SITUATIONS

Contents

HEATWAVE

Twenty-two days in the 100s. A record for Baltimore. Now, when I tell you I do not like to get hot. I do not like to get hot.

As if the weather wasn't enough, my niece Kiara was going through it. Dealing with this man she claims she wants to marry. Calling me every other night with some DE&I. Drama, Emergencies & Issues. Chile. But she's like a daughter to me. My only. So you know I was going through it, too.

Then a power transformer got the nerve to fail and take out electricity downtown. At rush hour. No traffic signals. At. Rush. Hour. People in this city already drive crazy, and there I was stuck in it. The chaotic head-lights and dark streets, it was too much.

My knuckles hurt from gripping the steering wheel. The news said BGE was working on it. Mechanical issue. I didn't care if it was biblical. All I know is my fifteen minute commute from the university took an hour-and-a-half. We only put it together later. Things would get worse.

But when I got home that night, all I wanted was my central air at 65 degrees, an episode of NCIS, and my leftover curry. And I was happy having all of that when the phone rang. Kiara. I started raising her when she was six, and I promised to always answer when she called. She'll be 33 in March.

I put down my spoonful of curry, (you know that last good bite), and pressed accept.

"Aunt Dee."

I knew from the shake in her voice that it was about him again, the fiancé. I turned off the TV, made myself a nook in the couch and put the phone on speaker in my lap. This was gonna be one of those.

"Davon's gone. " Her voice cracked.

No need to ask what she meant. I didn't
know exactly when it would end, but they
had some moments. Let's put it that way.

"We uh — ", she clipped her words. "We
got into it. I told him I didn't want to marry
him."

"You told him?" I sounded too surprised,
and instantly regretted it. But I already
knew she didn't want to marry him. And she
was in denial about it. Her next question
still caught me off guard.

"Why'd you say it like that?"

"I mean, you seemed happy."

We both knew I was lying. You couldn't
say Davon was outright domineering. But
he was serious. Had an idea about things.
And he was a lawyer, lord. Could shape any
conversation his way. But the thing is, Kiara
has never fit in anybody's shape. I brought
up the tension once, gently, and she let me

know "everything was fine" in a way that made me avoid the topic after that.

Deep in the couch, watching the last of my curry get cold, I could almost feel Kiara's tears dripping into the receiver. I felt like I was leaving her hanging. I felt that way around her a lot. Even when she was young. Nothing she ever did outright. Just little ways she'd let me know she wanted more. Expected more. The start she got to life, I couldn't blame her.

But it still hurt. I was feeling that dull pain when her laughter startled me. A weird short burst, like a machine gun.

"Do you know he took the ring?"

I wasn't surprised. He could be petty, dramatic.

I was trying not to say that out loud when my lights cut out. My central air powered down and the vents went quiet. The house was too silent without the AC running.
If you can't tell already, I love that girl like I

gave birth to her myself. But I Do. Not. Like to get hot.

So yes, I was distracted when she asked me if I'd heard what she said about the ring. And when I finally answered that my power had just gone out, she said I should probably save my phone battery. Short. A little attitude.

I offered to come over, and to keep talking on the phone — both twice before taking no for an answer. She didn't want me driving late. It had been a weird day. We both agreed on that. She was silent on the line, lingering.

"You there? You okay?"

"I'm fine. Are you okay?"

I told her what I always said. As long as she was good, then I was good. But I had to ask.

"What was it about, Kiara?"

"The boat."

"The boat?"

Davon had recently bought a Beneteau, even though he didn't sail. I think it was to keep pace with the other partners at the firm. (But that was another thing I couldn't bring up).

Kiara made an ugly sound that was almost a snort. "I told him I should have a key just in case. And he said just in case what? I said that's what just in case means. You don't know — it's just in case. We went back and forth, and it blew up. And he ended up walking out. It was so small", she gave another machine gun laugh that made me jump, "but the little things point to the big ones. Better now than later when there's more than just the two of us."

I noticed that phrase 'more than just the two of us', but I didn't touch it.

"Where did he go?"

"I don't know. But wherever he is, he can stay."

She said it so calmly after all that crying, I thought someone else was on the line. But she had said things like that before. And yet, here we were.

"Anyway, save your phone battery." That was her way of saying goodbye.

That night I prayed for Kiara (and Davon), and for the air to come back on.

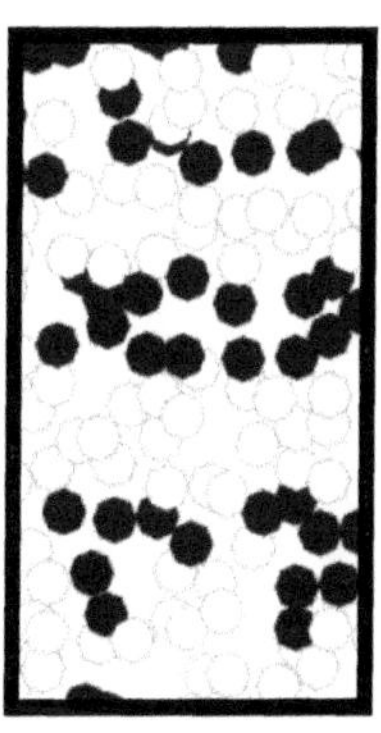

When my alarm went off, I was sweating like a Costco chicken. The power never came back on, and I had just been lying there with my eyes closed, hoping sleep would relieve me from the heat. It did not. When I opened my eyes, they focused on the motionless ceiling fan. I felt mocked. I peeled off my soaked cotton pajama top and picked up the phone. 6 AM.

Overnight, somebody sent me a TikTok of wildfires that had started in the counties surrounding the city. Scary. The trees on fire on each side of 95 made the four lane highway look like a cramped hall in a burning building.

I had opened my bedroom windows before going to bed, and I noticed that, yes, I could smell smoke. Even taste it a little. It was nasty, like someone down the block grilling burger packaging instead of meat. I had never heard of wildfires in Baltimore.

The Weather was calling for more heat, too — mhm — plus low air quality because of the fires. They were saying to shelter in place, in case of evacuation. But evacuation was a long shot.

The county might evacuate, but I felt like
Baltimore proper didn't have enough trees
to really burn. And there was no way I was
sitting in that smoky house with no AC.

I led a research center that was connected to
a university hospital. And the hospital had a
backup grid of its own. (And HEPA-filtered
central air). Plus, Kiara was right after all.
I needed to charge my phone. So I took a
cold shower, and drove myself right into
that office. The day was windy and dry,
like somebody waving a blow dryer in your
face. Back again behind the wheel of the
car where I had spent over an hour in traffic
the night before, I felt tired and annoyed at
everything.

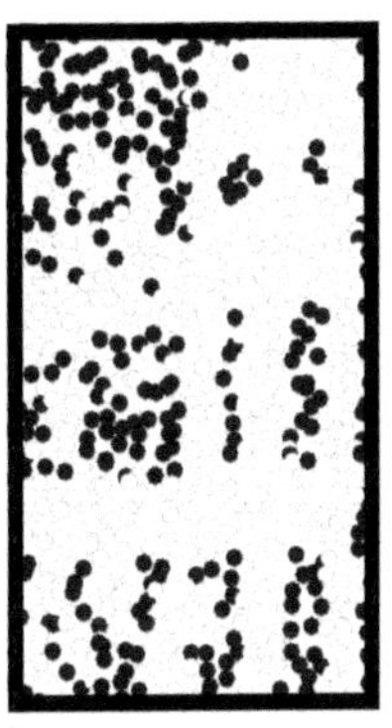

I knew something was off at the office as soon as the heavy glass door closed behind me. A few people were bunched around a monitor watching a YouTube video. Others throughout the room had the same video on their own screens, but from different websites. Everyone looked ragged. Like people who had run to work for refuge from smoke, sleepless nights, and cold showers. Just like me.

"There was an attack." The voice came from the big group. I joined them, stood over someone's shoulder and watched them replay the video.

It showed a man chasing a woman through the city. A round short woman in a pink cardigan. The man moved fast but full of jerks and ticks that made him look like he was in fast-forward. He had a ragged bouquet of flowers with petals missing and torn paper hanging down. Whoever made the video hid behind a line of cars, and the angle was terrible. You could see glimpses of shattered storefronts, and black smoke from a burning car engine. The woman in the sweater was huffing in her khakis. You know that game Kirby? A little pink balloon-looking thing.

Kiara used to love that game. That's what the lady in the pink sweater looked like to me, Kirby. I don't know why my brain is like that. She was screaming "I'm sorry! I'm sorry!" all out of breath.

The angle of the video shifted, and I almost fell out when I recognized the man in the video. Davon. He was bleeding from his ears and eyes and mouth. His face was stuck in a cry, like a photograph. And that face will forever be imprinted in my brain just like a photograph. The pain.

The five-foot-nothing woman is just a few paces in front of him; Davon is lunging for her hair, and his fingertips are touching the edge of her gray-blonde bob. The next part made my stomach turn.

Just as Davon got a good clutch of the woman's hair, a man jumped from an alley and brought a bat down on his collar bone. You could hear the crack. The arm holding the flowers went limp, but he didn't drop them. The Kirby lady took the chance to cut down an alley.

Before the man could swing again, Davon

choked him, bit his neck and tore it open like a human Pez Dispenser. The bat hit the pavement first. Then the man, trying to keep his neck from dripping through his fingers. Davon whipped around and looked directly at camera. Then he ran after the woman in the direction of downtown, flower petals flying everywhere. End of video.

I refused to believe it. I plopped down at my desk, and bounced around to different websites. YouTube, The Guardian, The Times, CNN, FoxNews; all of them had it as their main video: Baltimore Nerve Agent Exposure. Potential Terrorist Attack. My fingers automatically scrolled to the comments. I wished they hadn't. The comment with the most likes: Welp, this is the end. Can I get a @RedLobster Cheddar Biscuit for the road? And the second most: CNN. MSNBC. FOX. PROPAGANDA FOR ONE MEGACORP.

I read more about the nerve agent. They were calling it Agent Cimex. Because it was a black market version of Novichok that had been cut with bed bug saliva to make victims bleed more and faster. The target was unclear. Toy drones sprayed an entire neighborhood. Everyone else who was exposed

died. But somehow Davon survived. Disfig-
ured, bloodthirsty, but alive.

I pushed my chair away from the desk; I
was dizzy with questions. Kiara. Was she in
the attack? What if she was with Davon? I
grabbed my phone and saw a notification
screen full of missed calls. Another one in-
coming. Thank God. I answered.

"Are you okay?"

"Are you okay? I called you like ten times."

"There's something happening." I felt like I
needed to defend myself.

"I know. That's why I was calling you."

"You saw the video?"

She was quiet. I knew she had seen it.

People in the office talked over each other.
Panic. We weren't far from the attack.

"Where are you?"

I ducked to a quieter corner of the office.

"I'm at the center."

A sigh. "You were supposed to stay home."

"I didn't have AC."

"You said you would call me in the morning."

"It's 9 AM." I felt like I needed to defend myself again.

"We need to get out of the city. You should've stayed home. "

She was right. We both lived on the West Side, and the university is across town. She was right about leaving, too. She had learned the signs from me. The power. The wildfires. The attack. They were random-like. But not random. I knew because events like that were precisely what our research at the center was about.

Even though Kiara was right, I was tired and cranky and not in the mood for her special brand of intensity.

"I don't need you to tell me what to do, Kiara. I've lived a while."

It was awful timing. But it just came out.

"What do you mean, Aunt Dee?"

"I just mean it's been a tough couple days, and I'm irritated."

"With me?"

The hole was getting deeper. There was nothing right to say.

"No, not with you."

"But it sounds like it's me specifically. I can't help all this is happening to me."

"It's not just you, Kiara!"

I said it loud enough that people in the office looked over to my corner. I gave them a nod and stiff smile to tell them to mind their business.

The next thing Kiara said was muffled by static on the line. I got a text message that I ignored. Then another. And another. Another. A steady flood that made my phone vibrate like a toy. I heard other phones around the office beeping, buzzing, ringing. My call with Kiara dropped. I tried dialing again, but I kept getting texts about the #1 Male Enhancement Pill. My home screen wouldn't open. I turned my phone off and on again to see if I could get a call through. No.

"It's a TDos & SMS flood."

The grad student who runs our data science practice said that.

"What?" I had to raise my voice over the racket of phones.

"Someone is flooding the phone carrier networks with junk traffic, so regular calls can't get through. Eventually the network will crash."

As soon as he said that, and not a second later the phones stopped. I mean the last syllable was still clinging to his lip skin when the office went quiet. Whoo. Like all of it, the timing was so strange. I looked down at my phone. No signal. I had the thought I might never see Kiara again. That was the first time I remember feeling really afraid.

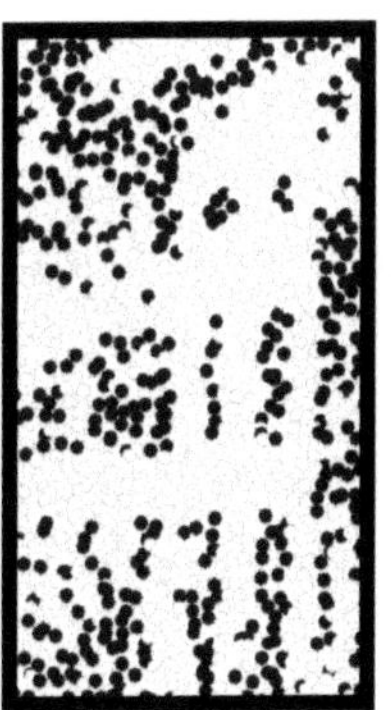

I looked at my colleagues. They weren't the same people I saw everyday. We were all raw with fear.

Fewer than a handful of people around the world really understood what was happening. And half of those were in the office with me.

The research center was technically part of an epidemiology lab. The main lab studied average diseases, and how they spread — viruses, heart disease, cancer. But our work was different from the main lab. We predictively modeled how interactions between the environment, political systems, and even families and individuals contributed to thriving (or catastrophe) in the total population. The harmful effects of systems and social dysfunction spread throughout a population in the same ways disease does. That was the theory I developed.

Like almost any powerful tool, our work could be weaponized. And this extremely unlikely combination of the physical terrorism that ravaged Davon, a cyber attack, an environmental disaster, and infrastructure failure — it had all the marks of stochastic warfare.

Without getting into the Greek, it basically means you don't attack your enemy directly. Instead, you identify cracks in their ecological, political, and social makeup. And then you cultivate the conditions for catastrophe. You don't know exactly when it will happen, and you don't know exactly how. But you know that eventually it will. It is a statistical certainty. And with AI, finding the patterns was easier than ever before.

"We need to leave." I said that out loud to the people in my office, but it felt like my voice was coming from somewhere else. Because I knew I wasn't going anywhere without Kiara. I also knew from that moment, things would deteriorate quickly. I knew universities and hospitals were bad places to be. And I was technically at both.

People in the office went to be with their people, and no one noticed when I hung back and waited. I knew Kiara would come.

Kiara has always been wilful. I guess you could call it that. She makes things happen. And I've always led an intellectual's life.

I thought. I read. I traveled. I wrote. I gave talks. I brought Kiara along with me, even as a little girl. Whatever city we ended up in, she always seemed to know her way around intuitively. She hated sitting in conferences, going to dinner with my colleagues, and listening to our theoretical excursions while she picked at dessert and we drank. Eventually I stopped arguing with her. At 14, I gave her a smart phone with location sharing, and I let her explore a single neighborhood on her own. At 16, she had her own key to our shared hotel room, and sometimes I wouldn't see her for the rest of the trip once we arrived. We would text, and she would just meet me at the airport when it was time to leave. She never missed a flight.

Waiting for Kiara in the office, I instinctively hid out of sight, under one of the desks. Sitting there alone and still, I noticed that my heart was pounding. I was close to a vent, and I felt the cool air blowing on my skin. I breathed deeply and slowly, calming myself down. And finally, somehow, I did what I wasn't able to the night before. I fell asleep.

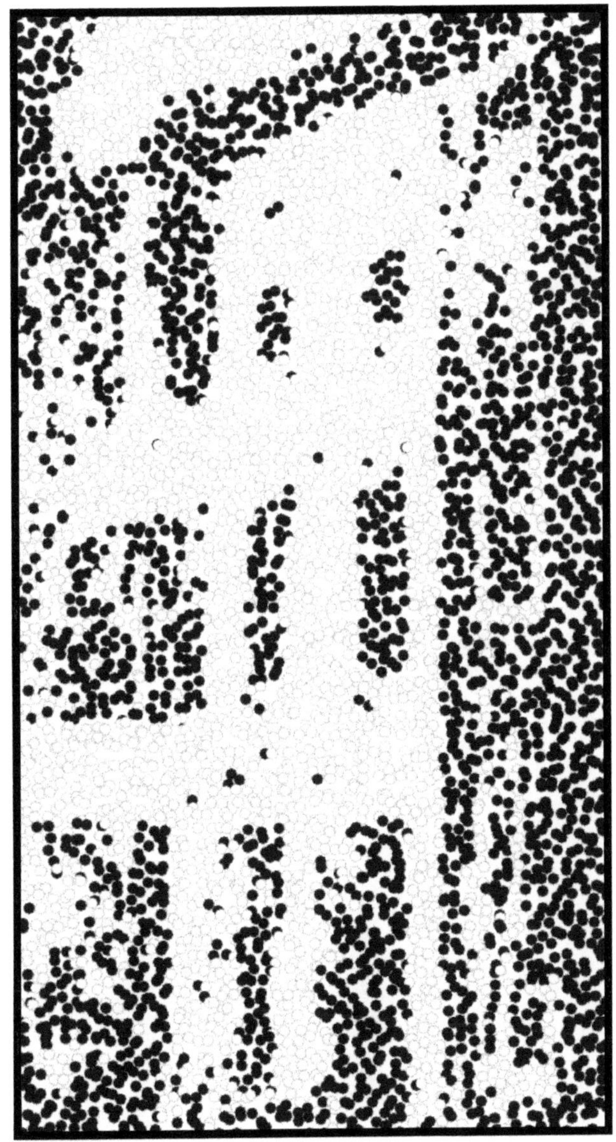

The sound of gunshots outside on the street startled me awake. I got to my knees and peeked out the window. Traffic was gridlocked. Wherever my colleagues had gone, they probably hadn't made it far in traffic like that. The gunshots stopped, and I couldn't see where they'd come from. Then I noticed a handful of police officers firing from the cover of a police SUV. I traced the direction of their guns, and saw that they were firing at another group of police officers, who shot back and dropped one of the cops in the first group. People in the crossfire abandoned their cars and ran, ducking low. I was only a couple stories high, and one of the officers looked up. I got out of the window fast. I was pretty sure they hadn't seen me. It was easy to deduce. Some of those police weren't really police.

I knew whoever got control would lock down the area, and it was too risky to bet on who was who. Most of them were white. There were a lot of beards and shaved heads. I heard something metal clanking on the office door. I peeked around the desk and saw several black Goretex boots on the other side of the glass. That was fast. So they had seen me. I heard them trying to force the lock open. They started banging the glass to break it. Then more gunshots.

This time right outside the door. I flinched because I had never been that close to gunfire before. I heard a keycard beep and the door swing open. I peeked in the gap between the floor and the desk, and saw a pair of boots enter the office and walk directly toward me.

I started crawling to another desk, but I knew the voice as soon as she spoke.

"Aunt Dee, I can see you."

I was wearing a long, electric teal sleeveless blouse. I thought I was hiding, but I realized the strip of color was easy to spot in the gap between the floor and the desk from anywhere in the room.

"Kiara?"

"No, it's Christopher Columbus."

I had to roll from under the desk, and get on all fours so I could start to stand up. These are old knees, honey. I noticed Kiara had a shotgun on her back with a strap across her chest.

"Since when do you have a gun?"

"It was Davon's. We can talk later. The fire spread to rowhomes. There's more of those dudes, and they are not cops."

Kiara watched me struggle up to one knee before taking off the shotgun and resting it against the desk. She bent into a deep squat and pulled me up.

"There were men outside the door." I was slightly out of breath.

"There were."

"What about Davon?"

"What about him? He's gone."

"Just like that?"

After weeks of giving me the blues about this man, she was suddenly so hard-edged. As much as I understood about what was going on outside, I knew about loss, too.

We both lost Kiara's mom. My sister. Even with therapy, neither one of us had really gotten over it. Grief can tear you up, and run you down.

There was enough going on outside. We didn't need anything else chasing us. The thing with Davon needed to come out. Kiara was quiet, just looking at me.

"You never even liked him, Aunt Dee."

"Girl, YOU, never liked him."

"And you never said anything."

"I tried. You won't let anybody look out for you."

I should not have said that. That set her off.

"Oh, it's my fault? I don't let people look out for me? Like you didn't have me running in the streets of Berlin at fifteen? It was always tenure, research, predictions, a new con-ference. You were too busy. So yeah, I had to learn to hold myself down. Some help would've been nice."

I noticed the AC cycle off from the vents above. The computer monitors shut down, too. Rolling blackouts. I started sweating the instant the air stopped blowing.

"Kiara, you know I would do anything for you. But that was the life I had to offer. Everything I knew to do, I did. Everything I could give, I gave. And anything I've ever had, has always been yours. I'm sorry if it wasn't enough."

I caught a glimpse of a figure creeping in the office door, and moving toward us. He was fast, agile. I picked up the shotgun, and let it roar in that direction. The glass shattered and the man in the black uniform fell. I felt a bruise between my breast and shoulder from the kick. Kiara was wide-eyed.

Fear and instincts were part of what made me pick up the gun, but the thought of some type of hostage situation in that building with no AC made me want to hop out of my body.

"Can we leave now?" I handed Kiara the shotgun back, "before it gets too hot in here."

"Thank you."

She said it almost too quietly to hear. It wasn't much, but it was what she had to offer.

A stochastic crisis is so dangerous because it's like sepsis. One failure triggers another until the downcycle spirals out of control. And the body dies. The population collapses. There was no way to tell who had set the dominoes in motion. And we might not know for years. Were the fires arson? Or bad luck plus climate? Did the killing squads on the streets have anything to do with the nerve agent? Were they homegrown white militias or were they planted, cultivated by a foreign state? I couldn't help thinking of these questions as Kiara sped through abandoned cars, weaving with the tires screeching.

I noticed we were going toward the harbor instead of the highway. Kirby and Davon had run that way in the video — deep into the city, with nowhere to go but the water. It wasn't an escape route.

"We're going downtown, baby." I said as gently as I could because we were barely on good terms again.

"Highways are shut down because of the fires."

"Then where are we going?"

"Put your seatbelt on, please."

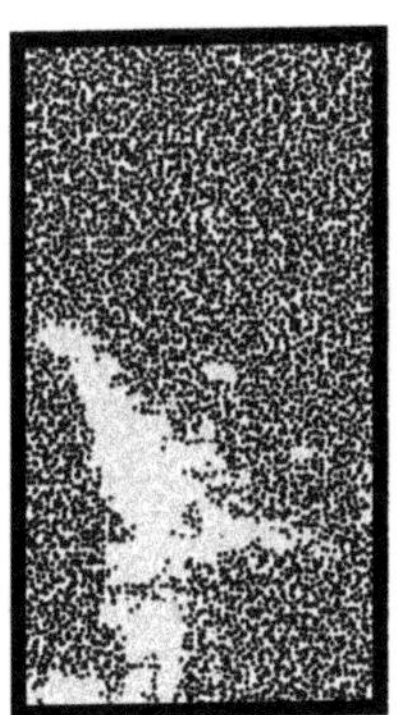

We pulled into the marina across from the aquarium. Down at the dock, I recognized Davon's big sailboat from the Instagram photos. Kiara could tell I was confused.

"I've been taking lessons so I could surprise Davon for his birthday with a sailing trip to Mexico. I snuck and had a copy of the key made. But then I realized I needed him to give me a key, so I wouldn't have to explain how I got one. That's what made the argument about a key so dumb. I already had it."

We heard engines revving and looked up toward the street leading to the marina. Police cruisers, black trucks and armored jeeps across the harbor and headed in our direction. A few minutes out. We weren't about to wait to see if they were for us or not.

With the boat's onboard motor, we could get out of the marina and on the river if we left immediately. Kiara was already on the boat messing with the rigging. I was swinging my foot onto the deck when a hand gripped my shoulder.

I swung around ready to fight, but I was surprised to see Kirby in her pink cardigan.

She was covered in dust and missing one of her loafers. She was bug eyed and delirious. Davon must have chased her all the way downtown. But where was he?

"I only asked if he paid for the flowers. And he turned around. And he. He got sprayed. They always keep the flowers in the front of the store. It's easy to forget to pay. I didn't mean anything by it. It wasn't a race thing."

I guessed she was talking about the tore up flowers Davon had in the video. But one thing I knew for certain was she wasn't about to get in that boat like she was trying to. She started to swing a leg over, and I pushed her back.

"Take me with you."

"I'm sorry." I did mean it. But she was not getting on that boat.

The lady tried pushing again and I was struggling with her when Kiara came from the other side of the boat with the shotgun trained on the woman. I prayed she knew better than to fire because shotgun blasts spread. I knew that from NCIS.

Then a bloody hand grabbed the woman by the hair and yanked her onto the pier. Davon. I won't describe what he did to her. But it was yet another photograph in my mind that I have tried (and failed) to erase from that day. Me and Kiara watched them struggle, and then topple into the harbor. They thrashed in the water until the woman stopped struggling. Then Davon's muscles went rigid, and they both sank, his hand on her collar, dragging her down.

The speeding police cars and black trucks were getting closer. I pulled on Kiara's sleeve. She wiped her tears, started the motor and got us on the river.

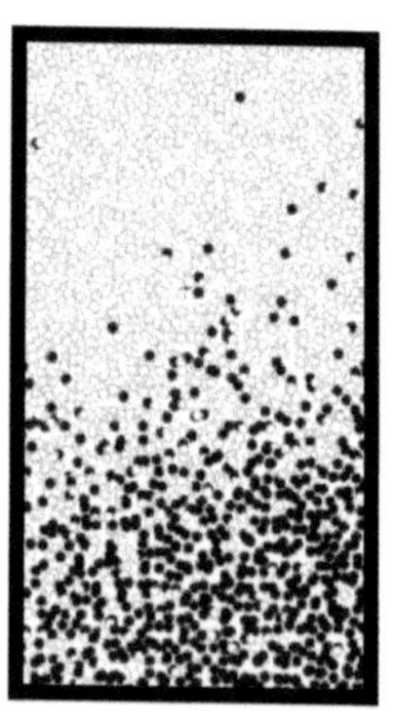

Out on the water with the sails up, the air felt cool and fresh. There was less and less smoke, the closer we got to the Chesapeake Bay. I filled my lungs with fresh air and felt all my muscles aching. Kiara was at the helm. I felt completely useless standing there next to her.

"You can go lie down." She kept her eyes out on the water, looking behind and ahead of us.

I was grateful, and didn't fight her on it. I tip-toed around the side of the boat and into the cabin.

A cold streak of fear zapped the sleep out of me. Someone had been in the cabin. The blinds were messed. The sheets were torn up. A door fixture was broken. Then I noticed a ragged bouquet of flowers wrapped up in the sheets. As sad as they looked, I could still smell their happy perfume. Taped to the flower wrapping paper was a note that read "I love you, Ki. Sorry."

There was also a blood-splattered ring box on the bed. I opened it, and inside was Kiara's engagement ring. Tucked into the same slot as the ring was a little boat key. I sat on the edge of the bed and cried. It's hard to predict exactly when things will happen. But it's easy to tell when it is too late.

I tossed the flowers and box through the cabin window into the water. I felt drained. I laid there with the window open, listening to the wind pull us along. I heard waves slapping the boat like a hundred drowning hands.

***

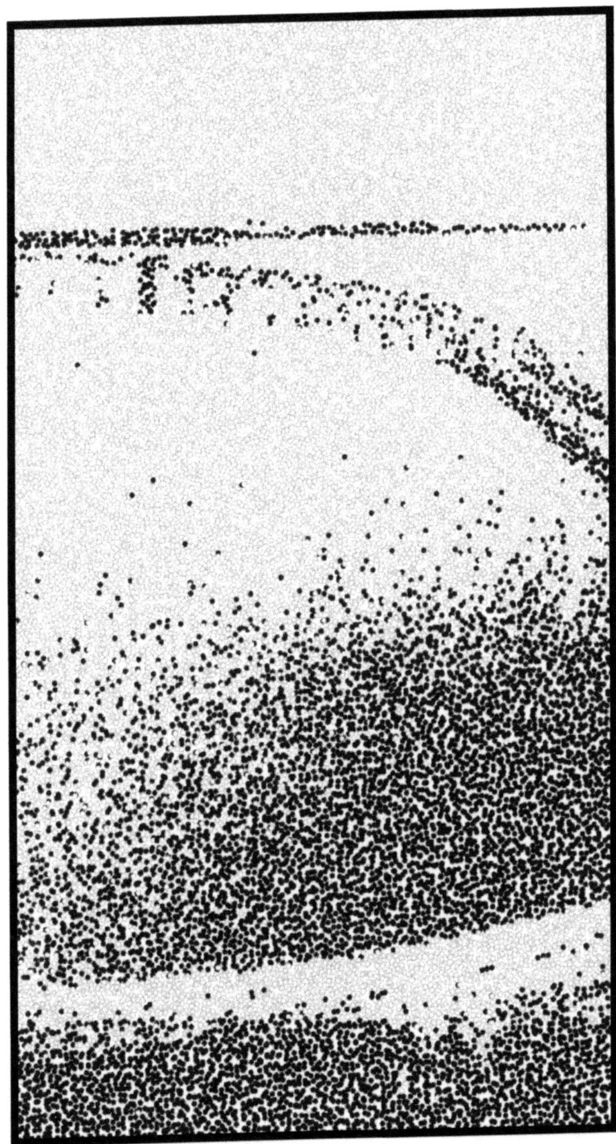

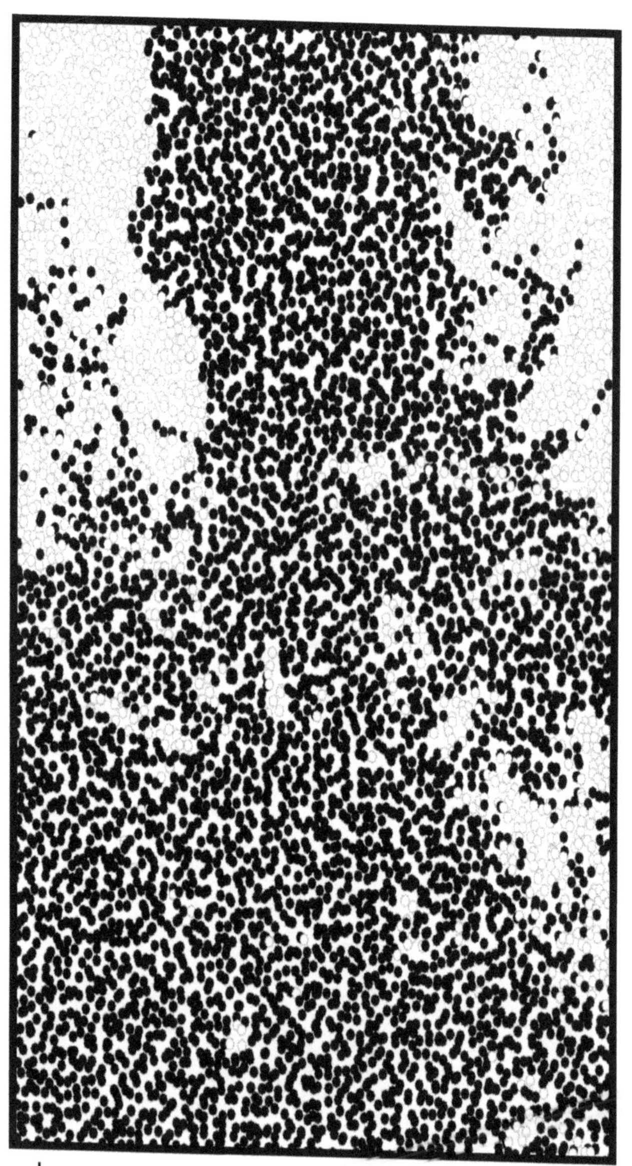

 | EVERYDAY BLACK PEOPLE IN STRANGE SITUATIONS

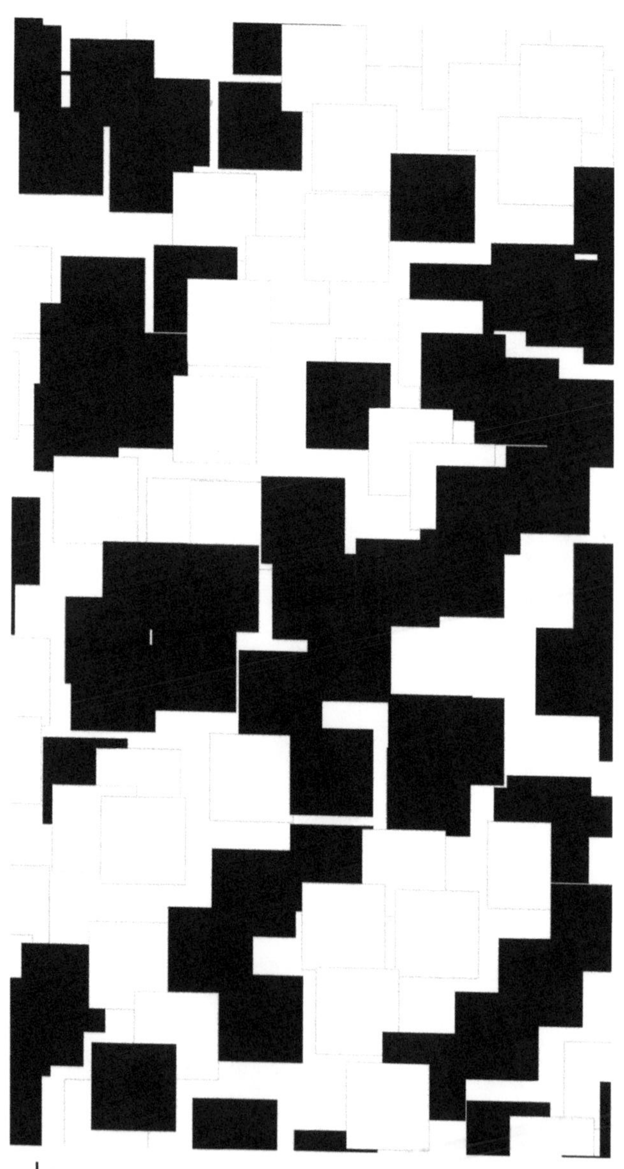

GUN

"You can kill a rat in all kinds of fucked up ways. But is it okay to kill a squirrel?" Kenny was on one. He threw back the last of his drink and waved to the bartender.

I knew better than to interrupt him when he got this way. Not because it would have offended him, but because it wouldn't matter. Once Kenny got going, his mouth was a noise making machine. From time to time he hovered around a point.

I guess you could call us drinking buddies. Put it like this: I can count on one hand the amount of times I've seen him in the daylight. Lately, Kenny's been sipping a little bit more than he used to. I get it. Losing someone is hard.

"You can kill a squirrel if you intend to eat it. But you better not kill a cat and eat that." Kenny tapped the bar with his index finger, like he'd just delivered the most profound wisdom.

The bartender walked up at the end of that last statement and was awkward about taking Kenny's drink order. John Wick played on the TV above the dark-glazed wooden bar.

The place was styled after an English pub where the bar wraps around the space so that most of the patrons can see each other. But this bar was different than other bars styled after English pubs because it was inside an empty Safeway.

Most of us were regulars. Kenny, me, Quiet Rob, the lady with the pony tail and boots who gave strong cop vibes, and the man with the big hands who always made references to sitcoms from the 2000s. An explosion made us all look up at the TV. John Wick — that's how we got into the conversation about what you can kill, and what's off limits.

The bartender's soft belly peek-a-bood from the bottom of his Orioles tee as he lifted his arm to pull Kenny's beer from the tap.

"You can kill a cow, and eat that. But a horse?" Kenny turned a questioning palm up, and raised an eyebrow.

"I'm vegan," the bartender placed Kenny's drink down and lingered for a second. Kenny gave him the silent you aren't a part of this conversation head nod. Again, awkward. Thankfully, someone else needed a drink.

Kenny leaned into me, but he forgot to lower his voice. "Everybody's vegan now. But they're just eating fucking fake chicken nuggets made from corn and yoga mats." He paused and sipped his beer.

"You vegan?"

I shook my head no.

We didn't go to the bar/Safeway because
it was good, or close by. It was actually out
of the way. We went because it was like a
pocket outside of normal life. It was across
the street from an abandoned train station.
It used to be a busy area, but it had become
a novelty — a place families took photos
during the day, and where kids smoked at
night. And where we went to drink.

Kenny lost his point, trailed off, and the bar
got quiet. A sad quiet that shined a harsh
spotlight on a bunch of randoms at a bar
inside an old grocery store. Everyone drinking for their private reasons. And for some
of the same reasons. This bar/Safeway used
to be at the edge of a suburban hamlet that
honestly could only be called quaint. It was
full of evergreen trees, and all the houses had a Scandinavian cottage vibe. Until
flooding caused the hill to slide and covered
all the homes in mud. That's why the Safeway went out of business. With the town
gone, there was no one to shop there. I miss
the village and the spiced hot chocolate
from their holiday market.

Weather like that happened more and more
frequently. And there were more and more

cheap drinking rooms like that bar, using whatever space they could. (Not exactly a licensed situation). There were also probably lots of Kennys with too many reasons to drink.

The night was losing momentum. A couple people slunk out of the bar and let a draft in as they left. I started to think about my own bed.

"She was everything. I miss her." Kenny swirled the little beer left in his glass.

I nodded and waited for him to continue. But he didn't. His wife was killed in a hit and run, barely a year ago. She was his best friend. I met her a few times. The sweetest person. She liked to go for a walk after her shift at the hospital because she said it helped get the smell off her. The driver was an elderly woman who said she'd thought she hit a deer.

Mercifully, John Wick started shooting again, and we all looked up at that.

Then we heard a sound that made all the sense in the world at first. Then it didn't make any sense at all. But it was an unmistakable sound. A train was pulling into the old station. It should have been impossible. The station had been abandoned for decades. The tracks were rusted, mostly decoration. And they stopped at a dead end a hundred yards in the woods.

Without talking about it, all of us in the bar filed out into the moonlight and crossed the street toward the sound.

We climbed the short hill to the station, and we all watched silently as a big steam engine, pitch black, chunked toward the platform. It kicked out big puffs of gray smoke that crackled and fizzed like television static.

Again, without needing to coordinate, we all walked to the platform and met the train as it arrived. We looked like a big strange drunk family, greeting the return of our beloved.

The train stopped with a loud hiss that made a few of us wince. For a long time, the train just sat there silently, with no one coming off. We knew better than to get on.

After a while, we heard a heavy Thunk, Thunk, Thunk, coming from the back of the train and getting closer. The closer it got, the more it sounded like there was a bubble banging through a gas line that was just about to explode.

Finally, the locomotive cab door swung open and someone appeared who was too perfect to be human. Grace Jones cheekbones, 7 feet tall, every muscle sculpted,

gleaming bald head and glowing dark skin.
And dressed in head-to-toe black leather. It
would have been kinky if we all weren't so
terrified.

This too perfect being stepped onto the platform, with two massive work boots, Thunk
Thunk, and looked down at all of us. In a
deep voice with bright bell overtones, they
said:

"One of you comes with me, or all of you."

We all looked around at each other, and
then Kenny said, "Shiiid, I dunno know
how your Wakanda lookin' ass got on these
tracks, but I'm going back inside to finish my
drink." With that, Kenny walked toward the
bar. He had gotten to the part of the night
where he was officially drinking for Her, his
wife.

"No." The beautiful one, the conductor, said
softly, but with certainty. We all watched as
Kenny's steps slowed, and his veins bulged
as he fought an invisible force, trying to
move forward. He collapsed to a knee,
exhausted after a good effort. Kenny's got
some scrap in him. We could see from the

sweat and his heavy breathing that he wasn't faking it, either. It took two of us to get him to his feet again.

"One of you, or all of you," then, "You have 10 minutes." It was a voice that spoke through us, instead of to us. I felt the base of my spine tingle like when close thunder strikes.

Right away the bartender said, "My daughter is only three months." I was surprised he had a daughter. He looked more like the loner Twitch streamer type.

Then the woman who was maybe a cop said, "I don't mean to be insensitive, but she probably won't remember you. My daughter's sixteen. She'll be a woman soon."

A man with thick gray hair that had thinned up front said, "I really feel like I just started living."

Someone finally thought to ask the conductor, who was standing nearby watching us squabble, where the train was going.

"You know where it goes." The voice was deep and final.

"This is crazy. We don't even know if this is real."

The bartender came to his senses and tried making a run for it, and fared worse than Kenny. Kenny gave running another go, and then I tried sneaking away while others argued. Moving felt like hiking through sand with a Prius attached to each of my limbs. I gave up and went back to the group.

The pony tail lady straightened her back and said firmly, "Law enforcement. You need to let these people leave right now."

I knew it. Cop.

A glimmer sparked in the beautiful one's eyes. A trace of a smile. "Or what?"

The beautiful one reached for their hip and the pony tail lady unholstered her weapon. But before she could fully point it at the beautiful one, she crackled and fizzed to smoke like the stuff that had come from the train. It happened so quickly she didn't even have a chance to shout. She just let out a quick 'ah', like she had dropped the cap to a bottle of Pepsi. The gun fell to the ground with a loud metallic clink.

The beautiful one took some tobacco from a pouch and rolled a cigarette. They started blowing puffs of smoke that also crackled.

We were all thinking it. The bartender went for it. "Does she count as the one?"

"No. Five minutes."

We tried running alone, and in groups, and I even tried sneaking away around the back of the station again. All our efforts brought us back exhausted and more fearful of the cool and absolute presence of the beautiful one, the conductor, the one in all black who had pulled a train into an abandoned station, who had arrived on a track that connected to nowhere.

Eventually, someone noticed Quiet Rob, who was hanging back by the seating area while the rest of us huddled and strategized.

Quiet Rob was always hanging back. That's how he got the name. (Of course, we never called him that to his face). Whenever we saw him at the bar, it felt like he was constantly receding into the background. He was shorter than average, wore glasses and always jumpstarted into his sentences in a way that wasn't quite a stutter. The few details we knew about his life came from back when we used to gently poke fun, like we would sometimes do with each other. Eventually, from his one word answers and 'wow, guys' responses, we realized it wasn't fun for him so we stopped.

The sitcom guy with big hands called out to Rob.

"Rob, my guy, you're single right?"

A woman from the bar with dyed red hair said, "No kids."

(She had drunkenly tried to put the moves on Rob once, and he rebuffed her. She was icy towards him ever since).

"I — don't want to go."

The three of them walked over to Rob.

"Let's talk about it."

"Rob, you could save people. Families." The bartender said that.

"I don't want to go."

"Why?"

"I don't want to."

"It's the right thing to do." The man with big hands grabbed a spot on Rob's shirt between his shoulder blades and started pushing. The bartender and the red-haired woman helped. Rob resisted, but he wasn't much for the three of them.

The beautiful one watched with the same amount of interest you might watch cars pull in and out of parking spaces.

I watched, too, in disbelief. But I also felt relieved. And ashamed that I felt relieved.

They were about to toss Rob headfirst on the train until we heard three loud bangs that made us duck. A handful of crows flapped from a nearby tree.

Kenny had the cop's gun pointed straight up

in the air. He lowered it so slowly, we could feel the time tightening around our necks. We didn't watch the gun, we watched his eyes. They were distant. And glazing with tears.

"You're right. Y'all have so much. You deserve to stay. I'll go."

The group let go of Quiet Rob, and Kenny walked between all of us. We made a path. No one tried stopping him. I considered him a friend. And I didn't try.

"Good," said the beautiful one, "Just in time. We have more stops to make."

Kenny boarded the train without looking at us. The beautiful one boarded behind him, the boots clunking and the long leather trench sweeping the stairs as they climbed. The train door closed with a clang. We watched it loop the station and go back the way it had come until it disappeared around a curve into the trees and we suddenly couldn't hear it anymore.

Those of us who were left wandered off one by one without looking at each other.

I went back to the bar, which was still un-
locked, and poured myself a shot. I had
another reason to drink now. I needed to
figure out what exactly did I have, and how
much of it did I deserve.

***

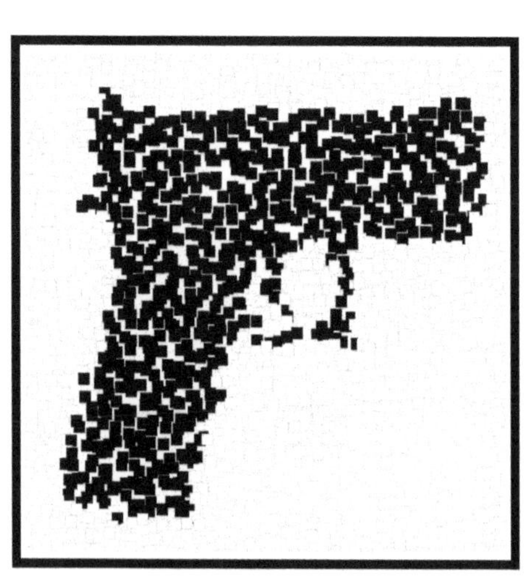

 | EVERYDAY BLACK PEOPLE IN STRANGE SITUATIONS

 | EVERYDAY BLACK PEOPLE IN STRANGE SITUATIONS

THE BEST YEAR

Before I tell you about the party that made me leave Hollywood, you need to know how I got the invite, and how hungry I was in those days.

I was so broke when I first got to LA that all I ate was crafty. I didn't know the word 'crafty' before coming to Hollywood. But then one of the staff writers on the show where I worked got me hip to the food — free food — that productions roll out for cast and crew. At the time, I had rent and gas fistfighting in my bank account, so the word crafty was a revelation. It was like a magic inscription on the back of an amulet. Crafty. You shall never go hungry. Àṣẹ.

The lot where I worked was massive — a city within the city. So big that visitors and important people didn't walk. They got chauffeured in golf carts with red upholstery and bottled water. I walked a lot, though. I had a habit of arriving early to wander until I found a food truck where I could slip in line with whatever production crew. Crafty. You shall never go hungry. Àṣẹ.

On the morning when I met The Guy, things were unusually slow, so I hiked to a far corner of the lot where I had never been. I ended up in the spot where they parked all the golf carts. It was in a corner with a bunch of props and rigging.

The sun was just rising, but the valley was already hot. I probably wouldn't have noticed The Guy, except his dark suit stood out in the flame-blue morning light. He was kneeling with his head slightly cocked toward the underside of one of the golf carts. Same angle as when my dad used to check the family car for a leak. (My family only bought used cars, and eventually they all started leaking something).

The Guy saw me watching. He stood up and rolled his neck with an impressive range of motion. I'd heard they do a lot of yoga in LA.

He walked toward me smiling with his hand extended, and we shook. His hand felt unusually warm, like he'd just been holding a fresh-boiled cup of tea. Everything else about him was so cool, though. Sunglasses, white shirt, great teeth. When he got closer, I saw from the wrinkles that the suit was linen. Not slick or corporate. More like a 'rich enough to be messy' vibe. His beat up white Adidas were the perfect punctuation.

He rattled off friendly questions like we'd just met in the grocery store wearing the same liberal arts college sweatshirt. What part of town did I live in, where was I from, what show did I work on, how long I had been in LA, and what did my parents do?

I told him all of it. He was cool like I said, genuinely interested. He dusted his palms and said it was good to meet me. Not many real ones like me in Hollywood anymore, and by the way did I happen to have any scripts?

I thought 'hell the fuck yeah' but I said something else.

He gave me his card. "Get me your favorite."

The card was printed on heavy stock with embossed red foil lettering. It felt important, like something might actually happen for me in this city.

I thought about how Pastor Roberts gave me a not-so-subtle warning from the pulpit the Sunday before I left town.

Since I was a kid, all I'd ever wanted was to write movies. I even screened my first film (made with an old camcorder from the church) in the fellowship hall. I'm sure the church folk thought I'd outgrow it and become a teacher or find a good job with the state. But now that I was leaving, I could see the terror and confusion behind their congratulations.

Soon as he got to whooping, pastor subbed me from the pulpit. He thunked a heavy palm on the lectern.

It might take years, ah.
Long niiights ah.
Isola-tion ah.
Sometimes, ah. Hollywood dreaeems, ah.
Turn reality skid row.
Silent tears, ah.
Patience, ah.
Stop and go, ah.
But Gaaawwwwwddd...

Sometimes people put their fear on you like

they are giving you their best armor. But it just ends up weighing you down. They don't mean anything by it.

After the sermon, Pastor slapped me on my back on my way out of church. It felt like he'd slapped a sticker on there that said 'fool'. And those first few months, that's exactly how I felt — like a fool. At any given point I was weeks away from crashing out. I didn't know anyone in the city, and I didn't have money for a flight home. The church folk were probably right to be afraid.

But now I watched The Guy stroll toward the front of the lot with the hot orange LA sun breaking over the mountains. I held his card, maybe my ticket, and I was glad for the first time that I took the chance.

A thought stopped The Guy mid-step. He turned back and called out "Try the trailers on Lot C. They keep 'em stocked with stuff for the execs. They don't eat it. They're bare-ly around."

I never figured out how The Guy knew what I was up to. I guess hungry people do have a look. I made sure my script got to his desk.

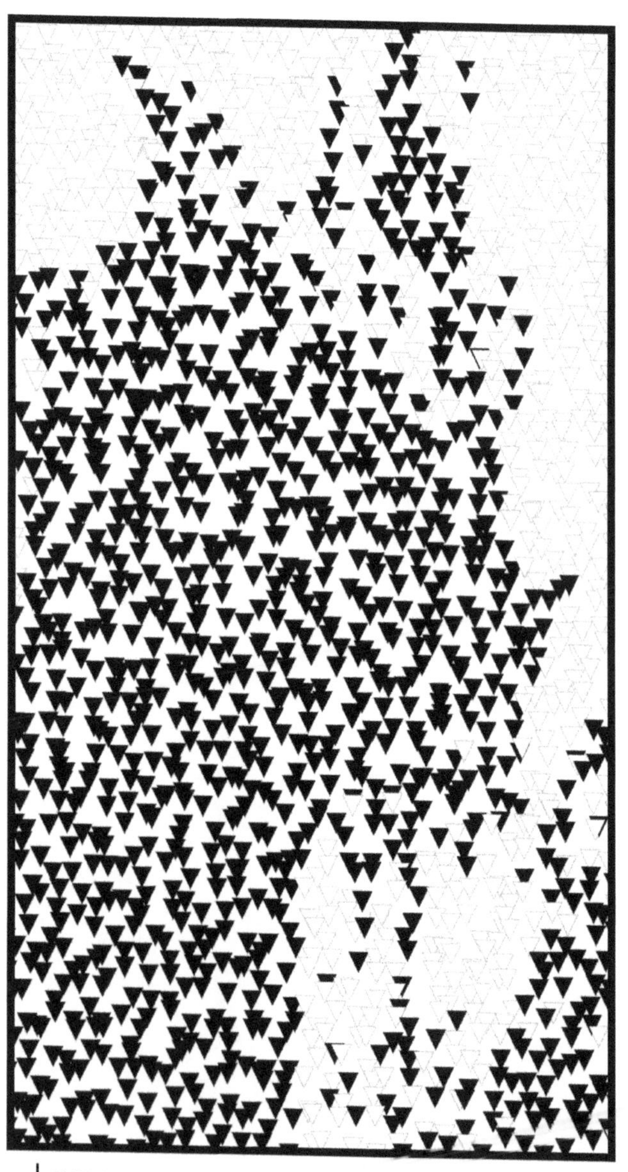

Normal day after that. I took shit, notes and coffee orders from the writers. In that order. I drove the hour home from the Valley to my apartment on The Eastside.

The next morning I was late. By the time I got to the lot, the sun was already shining on top of the mountain like the citrine centerpiece of a tiara. There were cops everywhere, plus a fire truck and an ambulance. The piercing smell of electrical fire.

I was mad because the firetruck was blocking my path to breakfast. The tip about the executive trailers on Lot C was good. The snacks were plentiful and bougie, and yes, mostly untouched. I had really been looking forward to a kouign amann, some scrambled eggs and fruit salad.

But I didn't have much time before the writers came in, so I settled for a plastic-wrapped muffin from a vending machine. The writers started gossiping as soon as they arrived. I pieced together the story of what happened that morning. A golf cart malfunction. Fifty-pound lithium battery explosion. Like those stupid hoverboards from back in the day, but bigger. Total body third-degree burns for the PA who was driving. And the exec who was being driven (seated in the back, directly over the battery) came out as bad as you can. In other words, not at all.

But the consensus was he wasn't worth mourning. The Tea was he somehow escaped 'Me Too', but was still as bad as the worst of them. Crazy how everybody in LA seemed to know about that stuff.

Time went on. I took more shit from the writers. I turned it into punch lists and lunch orders. Then one afternoon, The Guy popped his head into the writer's room. Same great teeth, sunglasses and rich-but-messy look.

It had been a while since that morning I met him inspecting the golf cart fleet. Honestly, I started to think I would never see him again. You could fill all the pools in LA with the amount of business cards and promises people hand out every day.

Yet, there he was. His skin was so healthy and clear, it looked almost liquid. He blew a whiff of salty air into the writers room, fresh from the spa, the beach, or both. I could tell from the quiet in a room that never got quiet — The Guy was more than just some corporate rando, he really was a heavy hitter. He smiled at everyone, and they waited for him to say what he was there to say.

He pointed at me, and then turned to the showrunner. "Have you read this kid? He's great. Someone passed me one of his scripts." He kept going without waiting for the showrunner to answer. "He's gotta be on staff next season, right? I mean…right?! "

"We'll talk." The showrunner was clearly upset, but didn't buck. In my short time, I had learned enough to know that the not-so-subtle nudge to hire me was taboo. Even if The Guy had juice, the show itself was the showrunner's creative queendom. And the writers room was her inner sanctum. Telling a showrunner who to hire was a big no-no.

The Guy tapped the door twice with his open palm and left. The room went from quiet to deeper than silent, like a mausoleum. I could see the writers doing the math, sizing each other up. There were only so many seats in the room. Adding one meant losing one. Eventually the eyes in the room turned to me, so I got up to close the door. It was part of my job, what I would have done anyway.

The door was slightly wet and warm where The Guy had placed his palm. I figured he had washed his hands and left the bathroom with them fully wet. He seemed the type.

Sidenote: The season when this all happened is considered to be the best season of the entire series. One of the best seasons of any series, period. GOT, Atlanta, The Wire, you name it. The New York Times called it 'generationally good television', and the show won an Emmy that year. Every writer was trying to save their ass by writing their ass off.

The vibe toward me shifted, of course. Things went from cool to glacial. And we're talking pre-global warming glaciers, hard as titanium. Not these new glaciers that are cracking up and leaking.

The worst of them was Tori, a wasp with a proper stinger who had come to TV by way of an Ivy League humor magazine. One time I made a clerical error; he corrected me making sure the whole room could hear, and followed up with, "but don't worry about it. You probably haven't been here long enough to know that." Another time he called my name and said intentionally too loud "I'm working on this urban character who gets his song on the Hip Hop Hot 100. That's still a thing right? For Rap people?" All with a smile, of course.

Other writers sold ideas, but Tori rarely did. He was 'more of a structure guy'. But he had pedigree and knew how to politic.

Time went on. I pitched a few of my own ideas. I took a little bit less shit since The Guy came in and vouched for me. I didn't get a staff writer role, but my shit job did turn into a slightly less shitty job making more money.

The showrunner pulled me into her office and sat at the edge of her desk. Tori was there on the two-seater couch. He had just been promoted to co-executive producer — second in command, but still a writer. The only place to sit would have been at the showrunner's knees, or next to Tori, so I just stood.

When they told me that I wouldn't be getting a staff writer role, I actually felt relieved because when the meeting popped on my calendar, I thought for sure I was about to be fired. Instead, they told me I was getting promoted to script coordinator. One level up. It flipped a digit on my paycheck and meant less grunt work. Good enough for the moment.

"We just don't have the space right now. But we'll be rooting for you. We need more stories like yours in this town." Tori said that.

Not long after that meeting, there was an investigation.

I got called into an office on a back lot. The faces looking back at me when I entered the room were all white, in suits, blouses, and pencil skirts so perfect and boring they had to be expensive. I hadn't seen most of them before. There were also police. The one face I did recognize mixed in with the muck-ety-mucks was The Guy. He was standing near the back of the group, and I realized he wasn't tall, but he had an unusually long neck. I know body shaming is supposed to be bad, but it was a weird neck.

I don't know how I didn't notice it when we first met. The Guy toned down his high-beam smile to something more subdued and appropriate for the moment. But still a smile. I must have been wearing my nerves like a diamond necklace because The Guy made eye contact and gave me an encourag-ing nod. His eyes caught light from a win-dow and glimmered.

They played a video of me going into the executive trailers. Even with my job on the line, I do have to say it was funny to watch. I looked left and right like a cartoon robber before ducking in the trailer and coming out with my head low, carrying four plates of food stacked together like UFOs mating in mid-flight. I couldn't think of something to say that wouldn't sound guilty as shit, so I didn't say anything.

"You're not in trouble," one of the cops said. I looked around at the blank expressions in the room, and it was clear they were too rich to care what I ate, or where I got it from.

Another cop picked up the thread. "But in order to get to those trailers from your place of work, the most direct route is past a bank of golf carts. We can't rule out foul play in the recent explosion here. To reiterate, you are not currently a suspect. But we'd like to know if you saw anything or anyone suspicious when you passed the golf carts. Did you witness something unusual the day this video was captured?"

I hesitated before answering. The day the video was captured was the day I met The Guy. Like I said, he was kneeling by one of the golf carts and looking under it. I looked over at The Guy and he gave me the most benign expression.

My mouth felt dry, and I could taste garlic on my tongue from the pesto pasta I'd just eaten. (I could buy lunch now and didn't always need the magic of crafty.)

I thought about the question. Had I seen anything strange? The morning we met, he could have been tying his sneakers. What were the facts? I saw him kneel and then stand up. That's it. It wasn't just a leap, it was acrobatics to turn that moment into something unusual.

Before his first meetings of the day, he took time to what? Rig an explosive device? Rewire complex electronics? He was a studio fly, not Jason Bourne. He was more natural wine and tranquilizers than intrigue and explosions.

No, he wasn't suspicious. He very much belonged to this place and to this group of people who were important enough to sit in on official police questioning. That day was a normal day. And something good came from it.

"No," I said, "I didn't see anything."

The cops asked me a few more questions and let me go. I must have been the last interview for the day because The Suits filed out after me. The Guy breezed past me in the hallway and gave my shoulder a friendly squeeze.

Already a few paces down the hallway, he called back to me "I'll see you soon, okay?"

Warmth lingered on the spot his hand touched my shoulder.

The investigation didn't last long; no witnesses, no evidence. The police went away. The writers also stopped gossiping about the dead exec. Life is weird, accidents happen.

I didn't see The Guy around the lot, and I was too busy with my new job to think about him very much. If we were friends, we were like city bus drivers who pass each other on their separate routes and nod. I did write him an email to say thanks for putting in a word. I told him my new job was cool, and even though I didn't make staff writer, I was working hard to land a spot in the room next season. He never responded.

The show wrapped production around the holidays. Writers went with family to cabins in Aspen, and beach houses in Santa Barbara. I spent the holiday alone in my new apartment (no roommates!) eating takeout and shopping online. I'm used to spending holidays alone. My siblings all have kids, and our parents died the year I turned 14.

I'm the youngest, and the year they died is when I first started going to church. No one told me to go. But around that time, I remembered how my grandmother used to always quote this passage talking about how Jesus was her rock, and a rock was what I needed then. It feels silly now, having been to church and seeing how people can be as slippery as moss there, too. But what did I know back then? I was a kid.

Anyway, I enjoyed that long stretch of down-time in LA, knowing the show had been picked up for another season. Knowing the 'starving artist' phase of my life was finally coming to a close. I went to Venice and sat for hours listening to the Pacific. I looked up at the billboards on Sunset and told myself the beautiful people on them weren't just stars anymore, they were my peers, and I was rising to my place among them in the sky. I ate sushi that came one piece to one exquisitely beautiful plate. I bought good Prosecco and drank it all. December wound down, and I was running out of ways to spend money that wouldn't take me back to being broke. So I sat down to do some writing.

Around 9pm on New Years Eve, I was home alone and planning on staying there when I got a call from a number I didn't recognize. I ignored it at first, but then they called back three times. On the fourth, I answered ready to sting. Then I recognized his voice. It was The Guy.

"You don't have my number saved?

C'mon!?" He did the thing where he talked without waiting for me to respond. "I'm having a party tonight. You'll be there, right? I'll text my address." Then he hung up.

I got there around 11:30. His house was in a corner of Malibu you don't know about unless you're supposed to. After driving up the mountain and pulling around the curved driveway, I was surprised by the small footprint of the house. A little disappointed, even. Except for the huge windows throughout, it reminded me of the split levels I used to see back home in Baltimore county. I thought my first Hollywood party would be a little more…Hollywood. I mean sure, I was in Malibu, but this place was as modest as the Amish. I opened the door, and then I understood.

A catalog living room with floor-to-ceiling windows overlooking sharp cliffs. An anteroom with a TV and a treadmill. A double balcony that at least tripled the square footage of the house. And the whole Pacific Ocean — ink dark with a seam of moonlight unzipping itself across the water.

The movie 'Biutiful' was playing in the TV

room. The warehouse scene where Javier Bardem's character finds the dead bodies of the exploited workers. Not really a party vibe.

I heard a Roberta Flack song playing on the supersized balcony and I walked in that direction. Through the sliding doors, I saw The Guy immediately. He was on a couch surrounded by a gaggle of people in various states of druggy euphoria. In other words, they were geeked. There was another group by the balcony railing, smoking and looking over the ocean. All very cool, very sexy, very Hollywood. This was more like it. Upstairs, I could hear the faint sounds of a few people really partying.

He walked up to me and hugged me tight. "Glad you made it. Found the place alright?"

I said I did. Again, my shoulders were slightly moist and warm where he touched me. But so many drugs can make you sweat. The reflection of the firepit danced in his eyes.

"Let me show you around."

We went to the kitchen and he poured me

a drink. The countertop was slick with who knows what. (Hand sanitizer?). He passed me the drink and smiled at me. It was awkward.

"Thanks for the invite."

"Of course, of course. You had to be here."

He led me through the house which was really a constellation of smaller structures tucked on the rugged cliffside. Not so much like those split-levels back in Baltimore after all. A sauna, an infinity pool, a Food Network kitchen, and a tasteful bedroom with a clear dome in the ceiling where the stars spun. He nodded to an ensuite bathroom and told me to wash my hands.

"Do a good job," he said, smiling as always.

That phrase and the too friendly way he said it — drugs or not — shifted something inside me. In the bathroom, I quietly cursed myself for being so naive. I'd seen enough TMZ to realize what type of party I had walked into. I wasn't about to be nobody's toy. Not today. Luckily I hadn't tasted my drink yet. I washed my hands and decided

that as soon as I had a moment, I would
Irish exit. I walked out of the bathroom and
left my drink on a ledge.

"Don't forget that." The Guy was nibbling on
a slider.

I turned around and grabbed my glass. I still
didn't drink.

We walked back up a set of stairs that led
to the top balcony where the big party was
going on. The balcony was half-covered
and half-open. On the open side, a few
people were lighting sparklers and tossing
them over the railing into the darkness.
The waves loudly struck the cliffside to say
thank you for the gift. The ocean sent up a
kiss of fresh salty air. It was almost midnight
and more people gathered upstairs.

The Guy walked me to a corner of the party
where the waves would drown out our conversation.

"Cheers" he said, and toasted me.

I said "Cheers" and he drank with his eyes
on me.

I took a half-hearted sip, hating that I put myself in this position.

Then he said my name. The first time I'd ever heard him use it. I looked at him.

"You could have really hurt me back there. In that room with The Suits. That means something."

I noticed he said "suits", like he wasn't standing there with them.

"I'm not from this town either. And when I came, all I had was my fire. You know? I see the same thing in you."

"Okay," I was distracted trying to gauge if I felt any different yet.

The thing he said next got my attention.

"You want to know why I killed that fat fucker? The golf cart exec."

We locked eyes.

"It wasn't because he was a predator, or because he hurt people. He was all of that, and he did all of that. It was because he tried to steal from me. What do they say on the internet? He was playing in my face?"

I nodded yes. Everybody talks the same these days.

"He was playing in my face. But you and me aren't like the rest of these people." He held up his finger and circled it around the house.

"C'mon. It's almost midnight. I don't want you to miss this."

He stood close to the railing and called everybody to gather round.

"Before we cross the threshold into a new year, I want to acknowledge someone who's here tonight, and I want to make an announcement. Tori."

I didn't even know he was there. Tori swaggered up with the confidence of someone who knows he's exactly where he belongs. For some reason, I had a special hate for him in that moment. One part of me wanted to jet back to my car, and back down the

mountain before this shit got any weird-
er; the other part of me wanted to calmly
squeeze my way through the crowd and
rock Tori's shit. For the quiet insults, for the
casual racism, for his shorts and sandals and
general lack of fashion sense.

Tori joined The Guy at his side. I figured
while people clapped and back-slapped after
whatever this announcement was would be
a good time to make an exit. The guy put an
arm around Tori's shoulder.

"Tori. You're smart."

Tori smiled.

"And you've given so much to the show.
You're cunning. And god knows you need
that in LA."

Tori beamed.

"But you're a shit writer. And you're annoying as fuck."

Tori's face fell. He looked confused. A few
people in the crowd snickered.

And then The Guy started to methodically strip naked, making sure to keep a hand on Tori so he didn't walk away. Tori just stood there looking dumb and made a quip that no one heard.

I took a glance around. People mostly looked bored. This was normal on this scene, I guess.

But the mood shifted when the guy's neck turned elastic. It started to roll, then stretch and stretch. All of us got quiet as his neck wound up into the sky like a wisp of smoke. It kept growing until his head was swallowed by the darkness. His arms shrunk close into his body. His legs fused together into a tail, and his skin turned translucent like rice paper. His insides looked like boiling red water. Then out of the darkness high above, a big blocky head with colorful scales, and three coal-glowing eyes snapped down and took off Tori's entire torso in one bite.

This creature with translucent skin, boiling insides, three eyes and a mouthful of white needle teeth. The closest thing I could compare it to was a dragon. But it wasn't a dragon. It was something I had never imagined, or wanted to.

Tori's bottom half spurted blood and collapsed. A few people clapped. It was Hollywood, after all. Great special effects. Maybe they thought this was a promo for new studio tech that would make us all lots of money.

And then the thing that used to be The Guy started snapping down from the sky and grabbing people at random, sometimes swallowing them into its boiling insides and sometimes tossing them over the rail into the ocean. People tried to run, but this thing was too fast and they were too high. Some people tried jumping off the balcony, taking their chance with the ocean and the rocks below. No good. The thing grabbed them out of mid-air, and tossed their bodies around like an orca toying with a seal. He spit a thick clear liquid that looked like hand sanitizer on three people in leather. After a beat they combusted. Then he ate them.

Fight, flight, or freeze. I found out which one I was that night. I was frozen, kneeling by a patio chair, watching the carnage, my

limbs feeling like they were made of wicker
— too stiff to pull up my body and run. The
thing that used to be The Guy kept killing
and eating and tossing. I watched it all until
he was finished. I blinked and cried silently.
There was nowhere to hide. I don't know
how long it went on. I heard crunching and
screaming and the waves and bodies on the
rocks.

When he was done, he took a winding flight
into the sky and burped a big Coca-Cola
burp from above. I could see sections of his
long body cutting through the clouds and
moonlight. He landed in the middle of the
balcony and roared.

Then he started to shrink. His arms sprout-
ed and became normal arms. His skin took
back its normal color. His tail split into two
and became human legs. His neck wound
down pulling a human head from the dark
sky that clicked into place between his
shoulders.

The Guy, back to human form, walked over
to me, naked, and extended a hand to lift
me up.

I looked up at him. "Did you put something in my drink?"

He laughed a big laugh that bounced off the cliffside and dove into the ocean. "No! What?! Why would I do that? That's crazy. No Diddy, my friend. No Diddy."

He grabbed my hand and pulled me to my feet. I flinched.

He put a hand on my shoulder. Warm, moist. "Too bad about Tori, huh? I guess a staff writer role just opened up."

I nodded.

"Listen, I'm tired now. You can find your way out, right? Same way you came."

I nodded again.

"Thanks again for what you did." He pulled champagne from an ice bucket on a side table and took a long swig straight from the bottle. Wine ran down the corner of his mouth and washed specks of blood down his chin in a thin pink stream.

He walked me to the front door, and as I walked out he said "It's gonna be a good year."

He took another swig and wiped his mouth. "This year's gonna be the best."

Then he watched as I started my car and drove off. I rolled down the window to let the sunrise in. The ocean smelled sharp, metallic.

Fear is strange. After what I had seen that night, it wasn't the blood and the screaming I was thinking about. Driving down the mountain, and away from LA forever, the memory that rushed back to me was from my childhood. I thought about a time not long after my parents passed. Upstairs in my dark bedroom, it was the preacher's son who showed me my first dirty movie.

***

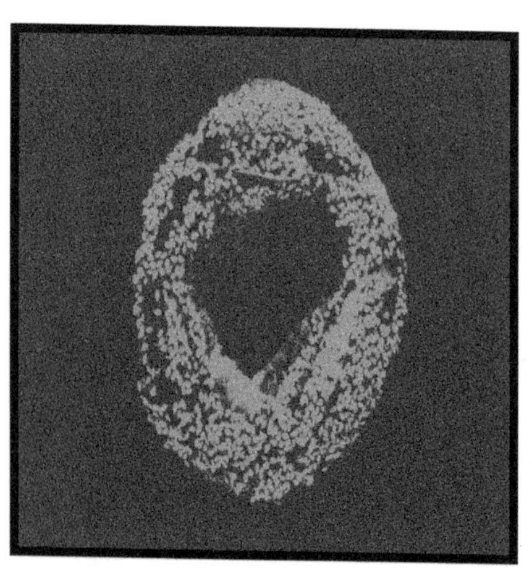

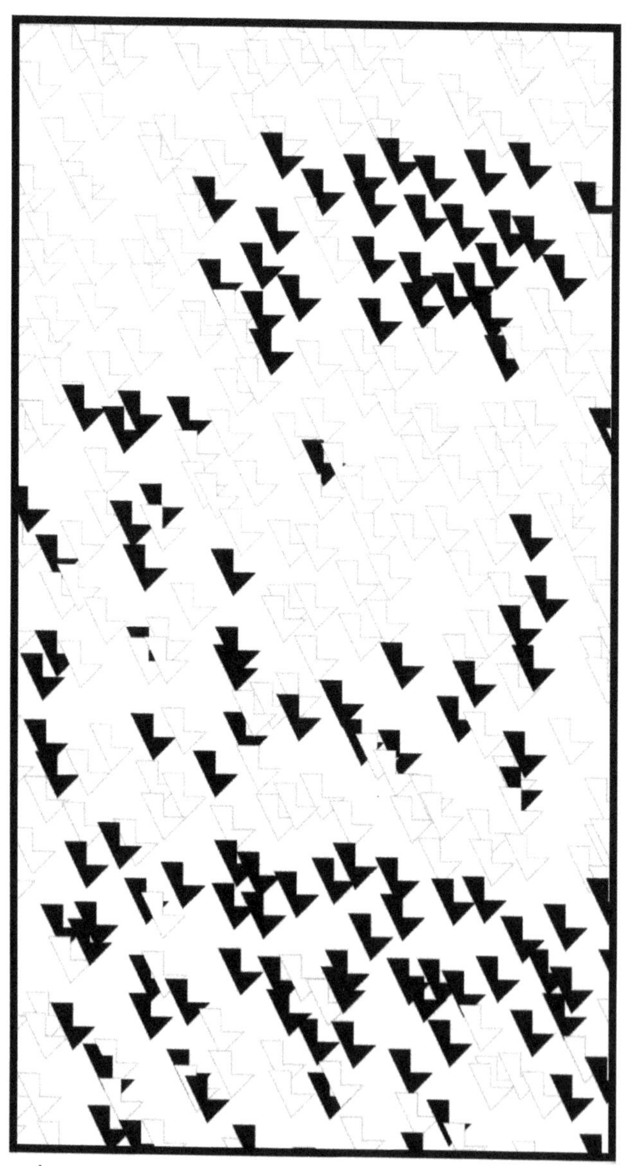

COLLECTOR

A buzzsaw red light jolts Shon awake in the Biotrac. After eight months down, her eyelids feel like velvet. She looks up at the ultra crisp display that blinks on above her. It shows a turquoise-magenta haze splattered with shotgun blasts of metallic gray dots: an asteroid field.

At 40,000 miles an hour, a collision with even the smallest particles could rip apart her ship's highgrade metal and leave her body exposed to the vacuum of space. In less than 2 minutes, her lungs would burst and her eyes would bulge like a horny cartoon character. She'll need to take manual control soon.

"K3-Larieux, baby" says the onboard AI, announcing the name of the field.

Shon's modded the onboard's voice module to sound like a southern granny who just ran out of cigarettes. It was a DIY job, so the accent is patchy at best.

"Should I call for help? Did she forget how to speak?"

The onboard's sarcasm doesn't land with Shon. The inside of her head feels waxy, slow moving.

"Thank you" Shon spreads her eyes wide and stretches her jaw.

Detecting the muscle activity, the Biotrac releases the GelWeb, and Shon's body floats in the dense silence. Her dark locs dance like Cape Town sea kelp.

"You're welcome, baby. You're gonna need to drive soon."

"How long?" Shon grunts out the words, clearing her throat.

"30 minutes, 24.6 seconds."

"You can just say a half-hour" Shon lets the words slip under her breath.

"And you can brush them fuzzy teeth of yours."

The entire cabin is outfitted with NASA-designed electret condenser microphones, sensitive enough to hear Shon's eyelashes kiss when she blinks. The onboard misses nothing.

"Got it." Shon uses a toe to push herself, gliding, out of the long transit capsule and into the cockpit. She straps into the pilot seat and zooms into a 3D model of the asteroid field on the nav display.

"It's dense. What's it made of?"

"Baby, you should have asked that question eight months ago."

"Could you have told me?"

"No, indeed."

"Right. So now that we're closer, what's it made of?"

Shon rotates the model and tilts her head, looking for the tell-tale signs of a resource-rich field — pockets of rainbow colored dots representing precious minerals.

"Don't know yet. Might be junk, might be water, might be diamonds. There's a lot of dust and gas. Like your love life."

"I just woke up. Don't make me turn you off."

"You got a message from Cris while you were down, by the way."

Tension swallows the cockpit. Shon twists her mouth.

Shon decides to ignore that latest piece of information for now and instead scrolls to a graphic meter representing her collection credits, which is how she gets paid. The meter is empty, except for a blinking orange bar above a solid red one. Shon is on a private contract to collect precious resources — minerals, water, volatile compounds — to keep life clicking along on earth. She gets paid on a bounty system where she receives minimal upfront pay and covers her own expenses. In trade, she gets to keep a cut of the total value of whatever she finds. For prospectors like Shon, big finds are exceedingly rare. But employees have the option of working off any debt they incur at a low interest rate. It's a risky job people work mostly out of necessity. The founder took his inspiration from a company that existed in the early 21st century. A company named after Earth's second longest river.

"Okay, using historical data from similar fields in similar regions, could you calculate the probable makeup of this field? Then tell me potential collection profits based on that makeup? Shon pauses while another thought forms, "...minus travel costs and company expenses."

"Sure baby. But what you're really asking is 'is it worth it?' And it's too late for that question now. You gon' pay what you gon' pay. You gon' make what you gon' make."

Shon looks up at a casino chip tethered to a ribbon between the ship's two front observation ports. On one side of the chip is the word 'Joy'. On the other side of the chip is the word 'Pain'. Shon and Cris each bought one on a trip they took to Vegas together. They got them from a street vendor because it was strange, and it reminded them of their favorite song by Frankie Beverly.

The chip is still spinning on the ribbon from the air disturbance Shon created when she strapped herself into the cockpit. Joy-Pain, Joy-Pain, Joy-Pain.

"Do the calculation please."

The onboard AI mocks a neutral computerized voice. "Historical data is unavailable," the voice slips back into a southern twang, "because no one told your fool behind to come 300 million miles out in space just because your little feelings were hurt."

"That's not why I'm here," some upset in Shon's voice. She regains her composure. "This is crazy. I'm not arguing with a computer."

"I got more bad news for you, baby. You got enough power to get to this field and run your shields while you analyze it. But you don't have enough to get home. We had to run the shields for longer than expected while you were down because of some unanticipated high-level radiation."

"So what? I just came 300 million miles to turn around?"

"Well, you can go there, and if it ain't nothing, you can wait for the company to come and pick you up."

Shon balks. "And how long will that take to pay back?"

"20 years."

"How long do I have to decide?"

"About five minutes."

Shon looks out into space and closes her eyes. Darkness on darkness.

"Play the message."

"These next few minutes could change the rest of your life, and you want to spend it on that girl?" Somewhere in its programming, the onboard AI was able to access the sound of genuine concern.

"Play it."

Three quick musical tones play and a woman's warm voice fills the cockpit.

Hey Shon. Hey baby. I know you probably won't listen to this, but I felt like I owed it to you to send it anyway. Not that I could ever explain what happened. Because I know it was wrong. And I'm so sorry for hurting you. It really was just a kiss. Just that moment. I swear that was the first time and only time. I know the timing was bad at your father's wake. It's just, I don't know.

"Say it," Shon says to the recording, to no one. A blob of tears breaks away from her face, and floats in the cabin, clear and glistening like a tiny diamond.

It's just that you can be demanding, Shon. I got overwhelmed. I got scared. I'm not blaming you. I'm just telling you what was going on for me. It's like that time in Vegas where you got drunk and forgot the number of the rental condo, and we went up & down like 10 different floors, until eventually I had to put you in a drunk cot from the casino while I tried every door until I found ours. And the next morning, you blamed me for not remembering because you told me to remember. I'm laughing because it was still one of the most fun trips, and I love you. I do love you, Shon. But I always felt like, I don't know. Like you wanted me to save you.

I know I can't fix what I broke. And I'm truly sorry for that. But I do want you to know. Whatever you're out there looking for, I really hope you find it.

More tears breaking loose and more tiny diamonds floating in the cabin. The onboard AI breaks the silence left after the recording stopped.

"I'm sorry baby, but you're gonna have to

make a call. What we gon' do?"

"It's like you said, you gon' get what you gon' get. You gon' give what you 'gon give."

Shon traps a floating blob of tears in her palm.

"I don't think I follow, baby." Somewhere in its programming, the onboard AI seems to access genuine consolation.

Shon takes the control stick. "We already came all this way. Might as well see what it's about."

Shon and the AI ride together in tense silence. Eventually the real asteroid field breaks into view. Shon pitches the ship sharply above it to get a view less obscured by dust. Below her, the field sparkles in a wash of color like a thousand-thousand Vegas strips. Cobalt, real diamonds, the purest frozen water, rare gems. Shon gasps. Joy bursts out of her body and she slaps the main dash.

"Can you analyze that?" she says to the onboard AI.

"Oh baby, we ain't finna work again. You want me to call the rescue team?"

"Nah, not yet." Shon says, turning the control stick for a better view of her new riches, "Just let me enjoy this. Someone will get here eventually."

* * *

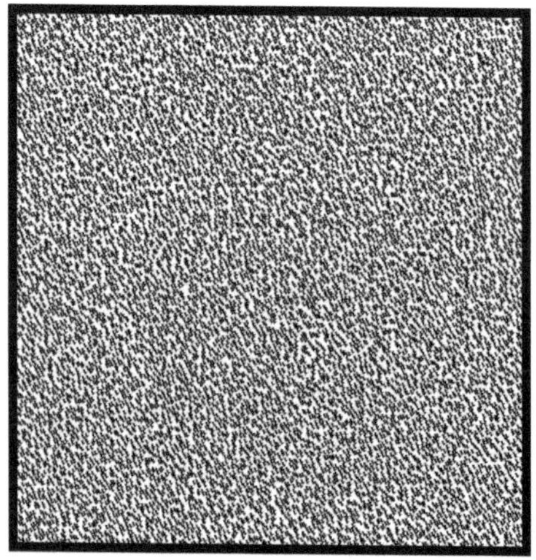

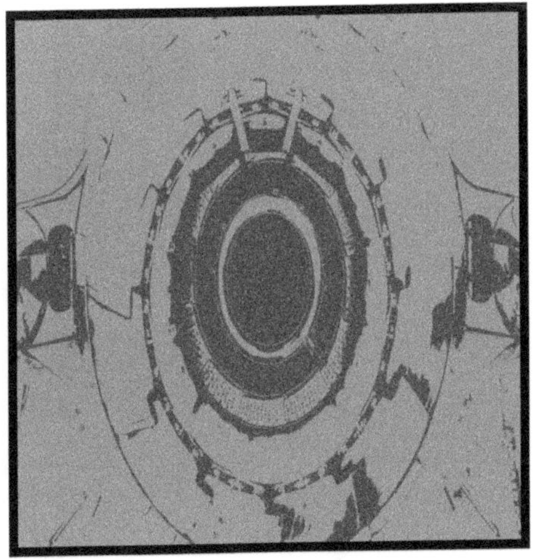

RADIO FREE GRENADA

Grenada. October 22, 1983

Heavy waves crash in the sunset. Humidity thick as a strawberry milkshake.

A soldier marches his prisoner, a woman, from the beach to the tree line. Her name is Jacqueline Creft, a leader of the island's young revolutionary government.

The soldier's boots crunch the gravel. He says "I wish you would have run, Jackie."

Grenada, a Caribbean island nation with a population smaller than Cleveland, has tumbled like a gymnast through the past day-and-a-half. Protests, riots, people in the street facing gunfire from soldiers and police.

The soldier says, "You didn't have to do this."

They cross the tree line. Palm leaves sweep over their heads and the air gets cooler.

Jacqueline raises her hands, "You're the one with the gun."

The soldier has sided with a faction in the revolutionary government that overthrew the Prime Minister, Maurice Bishop, because they believed he wasn't radical enough. That he was soft on The West. The idea seemed to just appear one day, bubbling up like swamp gas.

Jacqueline's last sentence is still hanging in the air when they arrive at a narrow pit surrounded by a circle of palms. The soldier raises his rifle and points the muzzle between her shoulder blades.

"You didn't leave. You wanted a family."

It was almost a question. He's reaching for some grain of sense.

There was an open secret that Jacqueline and the Prime Minister were more than revolutionary partners, despite the Prime Minister being married.

The safety off. The loud click-chunk of a chambered round.

"You feel proud doing this, what the Americans want?" Jacqueline is looking with one eye over her shoulder at the soldier.

They had grown up in the same small town, gone to the same university. The way their families told it, they are somehow cousins, though they never figured out the math.

An hour before the coup, the soldier had phoned Jacqueline to give her the chance to run. But she had already been warned by someone else days earlier — a little girl she thought was a stranger. She didn't believe it.

The soldier says "Americans nothing. Revolution takes sacrifice," trying to convince himself.

"Sacrifice isn't deciding what to lose, it's choosing what to have. All we want is a free Grenada."

"Don't be so righteous. You're no good to The People if y'ain't alive." There's both disgust and regret in his voice.

Jacqueline had helped lead the first socialist revolution of an English speaking nation. A

Black nation. Reagan, with the fire of The Panthers and the Black Power movement still smoldering, saw it as a threat. Because it was a threat. Too cozy with Cuba, what would happen if the Caribbean rose and called Black America to join?

The soldier says "I've never done this."

He waits for Jacqueline to ask, beg, bargain for her life, and when she doesn't, he says "Goodbye, Jackie," almost under his breath.

"Wait," she looks over her shoulder and catches his eye.

He lowers the gun, letting himself feel hopeful.

"Don't call me Jackie."

The soldier pulls the trigger, and before the round leaves the chamber, Jacqueline vanishes like someone turned off the TV and she was the picture.

On, off. There. Not there.

The fired round zooms through nothing and

cuts a chunk out of a palm tree. In disbelief, the soldier instinctively checks his back. More nothing. He turns round and round slowly. The woods are so quiet he can hear the space between the trees. The sound of a rustling monkey startles him and he sprays gunfire in random directions. When the clip is empty, the soldier lets the gun hang lamely around his knees.

Hints of moonlight tint the palm leaves silver.

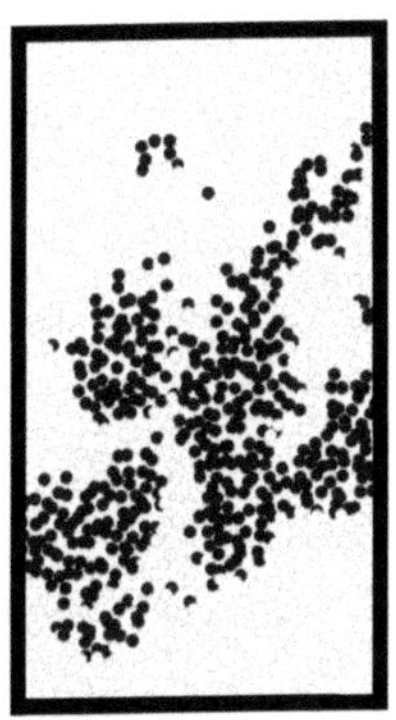

Manhattan. October 22, 2023

His name is Marques, but he tells people to call him Mo. He's finishing a strip steak at a table outside Bar Boulud in Manhattan. The bottle of Veuve on his table is barely touched. He's only ordered it because he wants an early taste of being the type of person who orders champagne like bottled water.

By the end of today, Mo will, in fact, have lots of money (less than Buffett, but more than Jay-Z). By the end of today, Mo will be something like dead.

In the meantime, he's drenched in designer. Dark Off White's shade him from the open-mouthed tourists wandering out of Central Park. He takes out his phone and reads three short lines.

Time confirmed.
Be at location.
Won't wait.

The text seems unnecessarily dramatic, but he figures it's a language thing. Mo is about to sell his business to foreign investors, some guys he's heard of through someone who knows someone who knows someone. An organization that's both above ground, and not-so-above ground, all led by a man called Desmond.

He hears they're from Turkey or Serbia or somewhere else in Asia or Europe. But as long as these guys have the money, he doesn't care where they're from. And considering he's also heard they'd be bigger than Apple if they actually had a market cap, he's pretty sure they've got the cash.

Mo spots the waiter at another sidewalk table and waives him down.

The waiter ignores him.

This lunch is a bittersweet celebration and goodbye. One police raid could have cost him years of work. One slip up, billions of dollars. One phone call from the wrong person who knew the right thing, and boom, prison. But now he's one deal away from a beach house and no neighbors but the ocean.

Mo's getting antsy sitting there with his plate getting cold and money to be made. So he uses a trick he picked up from the bros in FiDi, taking out his card and holding it straight up in the air.

It's an asshole move, but fuck it, he's about to have asshole money. It doesn't work. The place is picking up with a lunch crowd and the waiter jets inside the cafe with an arm full of plates, conspicuously not looking in Mo's direction. Mo sips a drip of nothing from his water glass.

He's lasering his eyes on the door of the restaurant when Mo feels a tap on his Botte-ga chunky loafer. He looks down just as a grapefruit rolls to a stop.

Mo bends over to pick up the fruit, and when he lifts his head again, there's a woman standing on the sidewalk looking straight at him. She holds out her hand, and he passes her the citrus.

Jacqueline says, "Young man, could you help me to my building?" She nods to her heavy red rolling basket. Inside are 10, ten-pound bags of grapefruit.

Mo looks at the basket and thinks hell no. But he just shakes his head and says "Sorry."

"Just a couple blocks. Won't take a minute." Jacqueline doesn't say it in a friendly way, or unfriendly. But she isn't leaving until he agrees to help.

Even though Mo is a stranger, she recognizes him. She can see the trouble on its way to his neck.

She's been through this tens of thousands of times since that night in Grenada. She's saved a pudgy bookish man from war in a far away future where big ugly slow drones crush people with stomach-churning soundwaves. She's pulled up a toddler from death face down in the mud. She has nudged a woman in an evening gown from the path of a speeding city bus.

It's always some person that feels familiar, someone Black like her that she can't help but care about. And they are always on the edge of life and whatever comes after. (It's still a mystery to her).

"I have to be somewhere." Mo takes out his phone and fiddles, keeping his eyes down. An image flashes in Jacqueline's mind of Mo being dragged into a shipping container. The interior is sound proofed. A man in a summer tan suit straps Mo to a dentist's chair. Behind the chair is a microdrill, a hand saw, a 3-pound sledge and some other deadly nasty instruments.

Seeing Mo in front of her, confident, yet blind to the painful death he's so well dressed to meet — it makes her feel tired.

In all the near and distant futures Jacqueline's met a few like Mo. Flashy, insecure. Genius, angry. Justified.

But still. His expensive jacket and watch.

His playboy shit-don't-stink face. It all makes her feel tired and worn down.

Jacqueline waits.

When Mo notices she's still standing there, he takes off his sunglasses and looks at her. She looks back.

"You can't help an old lady?"

Her freshness catches him off guard, but he recovers.

"You don't look that old."

"And you don't look that busy."

Jacqueline feels a little fire in her throat. She's surprised when she realizes she's getting annoyed. It's been a while.

The waiter finally brings the check and Mo signs it. He doesn't leave a tip.

Mo fully intends to get up and walk away, but his body won't let him. At first he thinks the feeling is guilt.

Then he recognizes uneasiness — like there's a cost for ignoring this woman.

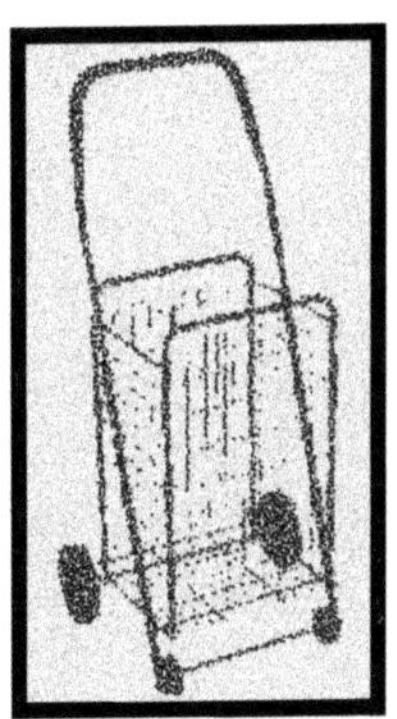

He checks his watch and gets up to take the cart, irritated by his own lack of resolve. Mo has to hustle to catch up with Jacqueline who's already a quarter-block away.

"How far did you say?" Mo jogs up to Jacqueline's side.

"I don't know."

And it's true. Her body tells her what she needs to know as she needs to know it. That's how it works whenever she jumps.

"Well, where do you live?" There was a definite amount of funk on the question.

"Just up here," Jacqueline stops in front of an apartment building. She isn't expecting it, but she isn't surprised. Again, what she needs to know, as she needs to know it.

Her hand flashes up and punches in the keycode. There's a loud buzz and a click. Jacqueline holds the building door open so Mo can pull in the cart of citrus. It's an old, narrow building and the stairs are steep. Mo gets the cart into the lobby, sweat beading.

The lobby is simple. A bank of mailboxes, a storage closet (with a sign that says 'Storage Closet') and stairs winding up towards a skylight. Mo still looks around and asks a stupid question.

"No elevator?"

Jacqueline says "I guess not."

She's never been to this apartment before. It used to feel strange, knowing things and not knowing how; having things (like an apartment or a cart of fruit) and having no idea where they came from. Recognizing details of people — a rhythmic laugh, an angle of the jawline or sculptural spread of the nose — and having no memory of meeting them.

But by now she's set loose from the type of thinking that time forces. She's seen a thousand ages and saved as many lives. It doesn't feel strange anymore.

Mo struggles up the stairs, with the bags of grapefruit gently bouncing. "What are you gonna do with all these?" Another serving of funk on the question, but also genuine curiosity.

"Not sure yet."

Jacqueline sees another vision. Mo, dead, tied up. In some kind of tannery — a warehouse space with soaring ceilings. An industrial lift lowers his body into a tank of acid.

"Going out to sea?"

Jacqueline ignores the snide comment. She's being patient with Mo, like he's a child. She remembers feeling sour herself back in Grenada when a teenage girl on the street asked her to help with the day's washing. Jacqueline looked at the big aluminum bucket full of whites and wanted to say no — she had a young revolution to raise — but her body wouldn't let her leave the girl without helping.

"Okay, which floor you on?" Mo's yanking the cart roughly up the stairs.

"Not sure yet."

"Look," Mo says, "I'm helping you out."

Jacqueline feels the fire in her throat again. To raise a revolution for the people of Grenada. A revolution that placed power in their own hands. Only to have it kicked over by some selfish men who wanted their picture on the cover of Time, like Castro and Che. Jealous men with an American president on an international line, whispering power.

Even though Jacqueline's been winding through, over and across time, today happens to be a 40 year straightaway to that painful day in Grenada. It's a dark anniversary and despite all she's seen, it still riles her.

The fire in her throat starts cooling when she finally accepts that she's just not in the mood for it. She doesn't feel like saving the day. Not today.

She stops on a landing and turns to face Mo, making sure he's looking her in the eyes.

"You said you had an appointment, right?"

Mo nods, "I'm selling my business."

Jacqueline hears the sound of Mo's screams from far off, like an echo across the valley of time.

"What do you do?"

Mo is as tired of this daffy lady as she is of him. So he decides to shock her with the truth.

"I'm the biggest producer and distributor of counterfeit luxury goods on the East Coast."

With a sing-song innocence, Jacqueline asks "do you have a business card?"

Mo is about to explain to her why he doesn't carry a business card when he realizes she's mocking him.

"If you go to that appointment, you won't get to spend a dollar."

Mo looks at her with thin eyes. What does she know? And what could she say that would make him walk away from a couple billie? And more than that, he's in a filthy business. The people in it make it that way. For too long he thought it wouldn't affect him. But now he can smell the stink on himself and needs badly to wash it away in warm Caribbean water.

He decides Jacqueline is one of the many crazies in the city, and he says so. "You're crazy."

"Do what you want. I've told you." Jacqueline takes the cart. "I got it from here."

Mo gives her a silent nod, and starts down the stairs, shaking his head.

"Hey," Jacqueline tosses him a grapefruit, "thanks for the help."

Even though she's here for Mo, she's fine letting him go. Only God knows Mo's fate, but sometimes lets Jacqueline take a peek.

Mo checks his watch again and feels annoyed because he had planned on walking downtown and now he has to take an Uber.

The car drops him off near Hudson yards, and while he waits, he watches the people climbing up and down from the Highline.

Precisely on time, a black Suburban appears,

a man in a tan suit hops out of the driver's seat and opens the back door. Mo gets in and the smell of old-world cologne floods his senses.

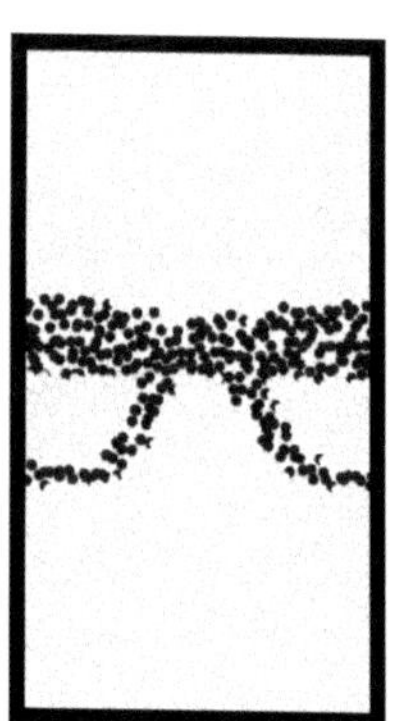

In the front passenger seat, there's a soft looking man with thin hair. This is Desmond. The driver gets behind the wheel and they pull off. Mo tries cracking the window, but it's locked. The three of them ride for a while in silence. Mo notices the traffic is light as they drive toward the Lincoln tunnel.

"Mind if I open the window?"

Desmond ignores the question.

"Mr. Marques, it's unusual to arrange a deal of this size on such short notice. I'm sure you have your reasons."

Mo has his reasons, but he's not about to get into them.

"You can call me Mo."

"Would you like to know why we agreed?"

The cologne is starting to make Mo feel slightly nauseous. His mouth is watering. He scratches the rind of the grapefruit and smells it. That helps a little.

"It's good business. I'm offering a significant discount on the actual value."

"Mmhmm." Desmond doesn't bother pretending to be interested in this answer.

"Mr. Marques, we're in the same business. You make fake designer goods. Handbags, belts, items like this. "

"I wouldn't say fake." Mo already doesn't like Desmond because he reminds him of the teachers in high school who looked at him and only saw his neighborhood, his fathers oily MTA overalls. The teachers who, without evidence of any cheating, handed him the A's he earned with a quiet disbelief, a subtle grudge.

"Yes. Fake isn't quite correct, is it? You are thorough, like me. You source your leather from Europe. You have poached artisans from Asniéres. Your product is the best on the East Coast, probably in the entire US market. Even experts cannot tell the difference. And you have, wisely, consolidated your competition. You are the Black Bernard Arnault."

"Okay."

Mo feels like Desmond said 'Black' in a weird way, but he also feels like most people who aren't Black do. He's also not surprised by the due diligence. Criminals tend to be careful business people. At least the ones that stay free, and alive.

"If not quality, what's the difference between what you produce and what comes directly from LVMH?"

Mo doesn't answer. He built his business up from selling handbags on a fleece blanket in Koreatown to one of the biggest in The States, with only a short list of people in the whole world bigger than him. Desmond is on that list.

"Provenance, Mr. Marques." There is a hint of delight in Desmond's voice, as if he's revealed some ultimate insight.

Looking out the window, Mo doesn't recognize the part of New Jersey they're driving through. But he also doesn't visit Jersey often.

"We're headed to your office?"

"Mmhmm."

A few more minutes of silence.

"The window's locked. I want to put it down."

The driver presses a button and Mo cracks the window. They drive along the Passaic river until they turn into an industrial park stacked high with shipping containers.

The driver gets out and opens Mo's door. Desmond is already standing outside with his hand resting on the headlight of the SUV. He nods to the grapefruit Mo is still holding.

"Did you bring it to share?"

Mo had almost forgotten he had it.

"Some lady gave it to me." He holds it out to Desmond with a raised eyebrows 'd'you want it' expression.

"No, no. Acid reflux." Desmond pats his stomach.

Mo makes a mental note to look for a trash can.

The three men walk towards a slab cement building, standing ugly and alone with only pallet stacking machines and thick plastic barrels to keep it company.

Desmond walks slightly ahead and looks over his shoulder to talk to Mo.

"We'll send payment today as soon as you sign. Our lawyer will be by later this week with some final paperwork. Small things. Do you have the keys?"

They've already negotiated the part of this deal the IRS will know about — the transfer of multiple LLCs, all registered in New York, from Mo to Desmond. And once Desmond sends the crypto to Mo's hot wallet, Mo will hand over an NFC tag with codes that give access to his entire stock across several different warehouses. For extra security (it's the careful who last), the tag is encrypted with a passcode.

"I got the keys, yeah." Mo's annoyed they had to do this in person, but then again considering the amount and the legality, he guessed there wasn't another way.

They enter the building. Big industrial fans whoosh overhead. The room is dotted with huge vats, and a slight smell of chemical rot wafts through the air.

"Leather processing" says Desmond.

They make a sharp turn and start winding through a labyrinth of hallways. Holding the awkward and fleshy fruit, Mo notices that for an industrial park, there's a strange lack of trash receptacles. They must be a green operation.

"Did you go to university, Mr. Marques?"

"No. Dropped out of high school. All they teach you is to sit still and obey. I'm not a dog."

Desmond laughs, "that's true."

They stop at a door with a cheap plastic placard that says 'Office'.

The man opens the door and goes in, followed by Desmond who invites Mo in with a gentlemanly gesture.

In the room is a window overlooking the shipping containers; Mo can also see the river glimmering in the distance like a jeweled necklace laid straight out on a dresser. There is a short oval-shaped conference table with a pen and two thick stacks of stapled papers.

Mo works his way through the first stack, signing page after page under Desmond's signature. Then he does the same with the second stack until they're both complete. Midway through the signing, Desmond excuses himself and his silent man saying they needed to 'attend to an issue'. Waiting for him to return, Mo picks up the grapefruit and tosses it up and down. He looks around the room, but there is literally nothing to see. Design inspiration: cardboard box.

Finally Mo hears the handle click on the door behind him, and he smells Desmond before he actually enters. He enters alone and walks to the opposite end of the table.

"Ah you're finished. That's good. And the key?"

Mo holds up an NFC-enabled fob.

"And it is encrypted, or…?"

"It is, yeah."

"And what did you say the code was again Mr. Marques?"

"I'll send it opposite your payment."

Desmond smiles a thin smile and laughs at himself that he could be so silly. "Ah, right. Of course. Then there's one more thing before we send you on your way. You never shared why you are in such a hurry to sell your business. If you don't wish to share, I understand. That is certainly…your business."

Desmond takes obvious pleasure in the repetition that is not quite a pun.

"But I would like you to know, Mr. Marques, why this arrangement is acceptable to us."

Mo hears the door click open behind him.

"Because, as I said, we are in the same business."

Before the door closes, Mo feels the air rush
out of the room, and the silent man's bicep
squeezing his windpipe. He tries gasping,
but only a papery sound comes out. Mo
kicks up from the chair and tries to struggle
to his feet, but the silent man tightens his
grip and sinks down low. Mo keeps struggling and sees Desmond walk calmly from
the opposite end of the table and stand just
out of reach.

"It was poor judgment to come here. We are not peers, Mr. Marques. Now give me the code, or this will get much worse."

Mo's eyes are rolling around in the room involuntarily. His hands are gripped tight to the silent man's arm, with no effect. The room is going blurry. Mo spots the grapefruit on the floor. It had fallen from the table during the struggle. All in one motion, he grabs the fruit, jabs a thumb in it and sends it backward wildly while squeezing hard. He lands it just below the silent man's eye socket and sends a spurt of acid citrus into his eyeball. The man's hand instinctively shoots up to his face, giving Mo enough leverage to shake loose. The man tries gripping again and the two men grapple on the floor like vipers locked in death.

As the two men roll, Desmond clicks open a blade and tries stabbing Mo. He misses and jabs the blade into his silent man's flank. The man's arms go slack and Mo scrambles to the door. Desmond lunges for the seam of his pants and makes him fall face forward toward the door handle.

Mo closes his eyes, expecting to rock his forehead, but just as he's about to make impact, he feels himself land on something soft. When Mo opens his eyes again, he's face down on a divan in a strange apartment.

"Breathe" a voice says. A voice he recognizes.

 He turns over and sees the annoying old lady with the fruit from earlier in the day.

"Get back!"

Jacqueline tries to put a gentle hand on Mo's forehead, and Mo slaps it away.

"I hate to say I told you so", she says, calmly taking a few steps back.

Mo gets to his feet and scans the room, feeling a little bit woozy. He spots the door and makes a beeline toward the exit.

"You won't get another chance if you leave." Jacqueline's voice is just above room temperature.

Mo stops and spends a long minute with his hand on the door handle.

He finally says, "What is this?" The tremble in his voice matches the one in his arm.

"It's a choice." Jacqueline motions for Mo to sit, but he stays in place at the door.

The girl in Grenada had given her the same choice she's about to give Mo.

"Who are you?"

The girl in Grenada had said specifically that she was Jacqueline's great-great-grand-aunt's cousin. Jacqueline opts for a simpler approach.

"I'm family. Someone you can trust."

Mo thinks about all the people who said he could trust them over the years — how that usually works out — and he turns the han-dle.

"Look. It might not make sense to you, but you're alive."

Mo is still in the apartment. The door creaks shut and he turns to face Jacqueline.

She says, "earlier today, why'd you help me?"

After a beat, Mo answers, "I don't know."

"Think about it."

"I was afraid."

"Afraid of what?"

"I don't know. A feeling."

Jacqueline nods. "A long time ago, I had a similar feeling. A girl asked me to help me with her washing. She said I should leave my home while I still had a chance. She also said she was family, that she was older than me. I didn't call her crazy, but — "

Mo recognizes the callback, nods.

"But then something happened where I was sure I would die. I was ready. And right at the moment —"

Jacqueline snaps her fingers.

Mo says "I don't understand."

Jacqueline nods. "I didn't either. But I'll tell you what she told me: it runs in the family. It's something that family does for family."

"How?"

"Dunno. You don't think about it. You just feel it."

Mo takes a seat.

"We're related?"

Jacqueline hands him a glass of water she had ready on the counter.

"Gotta be."

Mo drinks a long gulp of water.

"So what now?"

"You get the same choice she gave me."

Mo finishes off the water.

"You can go back to wherever you just came from. Or you can stay and help."

"Not much of a choice."

"But it's a choice."

Mo lets what Jacqueline is saying settle, without trying to move the pieces around too much.

"And then what — I save people from, like, dying?"

"Something like that, yeah. And not just any people. Family. We're connected across time, like a thread of pearls. We keep the thread from breaking."

"Does it end?"

"Everything ends."

"When?"

Jacqueline looks at him with the years in her eyes and says, "When it ends."

She grabs a big bag of Domino sugar from a

high cabinet and turns to Mo, holding it up.

"You want some grapefruit?"

Mo takes a seat and Jacqueline hands him a spoon.

Grenada. October 25th, 1983

Three days after he witnessed reality wrap an invisible curtain around Jacqueline, the soldier, her cousin, is taking heavy fire from US forces. After the coup, Reagan decided to invade Grenada "to stabilize the region and to protect US citizens from a dangerous communist regime."

The soldier returns fire and takes cover. He can feel the bullets whizzing past him like murderous wasps.

He changes position from behind the cover of palms and a bullet chunks through a tree, just missing his neck and sending wood chips in his eyes.

He lies down in a natural divot, certain it's the end. He thinks briefly about all the cities he hasn't seen. Then his mind takes him back to the farm he grew up on, cultivating clove and grapefruit. As he lies in the dry leaves, ready to die, he wishes he could go home again. He prays. An RPG roars in his direction.

Manhattan. October 25th, 2023

Jacqueline is alone in her kitchen, eating half a grapefruit with a big scoop of sugar. The fluorescents light up the palm trees on her wallpaper like an overcast sun. A thread of grapefruit juice escapes the corner of her mouth and inches down her chin. She feels a backwards pull in time, hears a whispered prayer. A voice she recognizes.

With her elbows on the kitchen table, Jacqueline taps her foot as the grapefruit juice runs down her chin. The moment is too sweet to interrupt. She finishes her own, and starts on the half-eaten grapefruit at the table setting across from her. She sets the extra plate and spoon in the warm dish water. Now, let someone else do the saving.

***

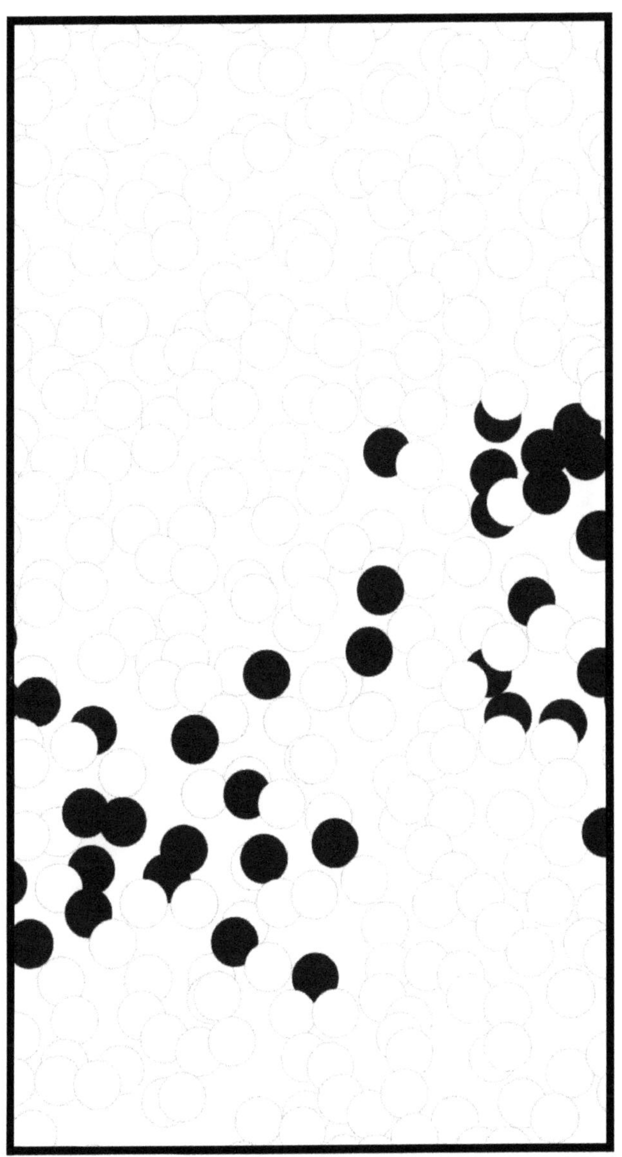

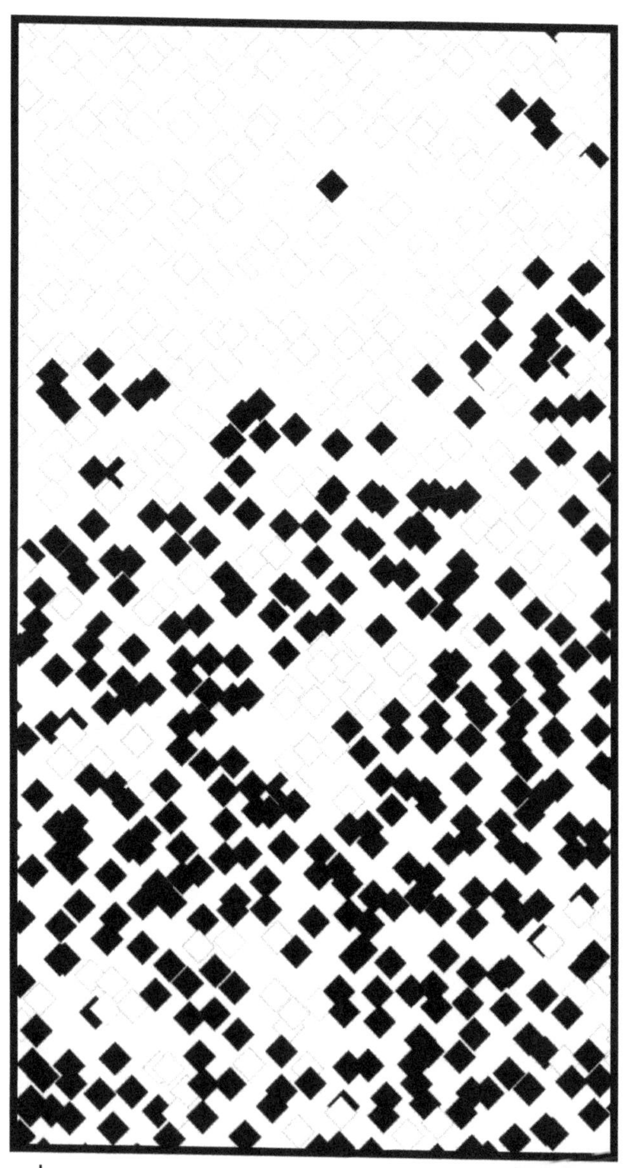

10 WAYS THE WORLD ENDS

1 // RA Khalil Earthborn, Oakland CA

To understand death, and my own so-called "death" in particular, you must first understand time in its feminine and its masculine aspects.

Time, in its masculine aspect, operates at the level of what the dominant power structure would call classical physics. (A system we know originated with the Kushites over 3000 years ago).

But time has another aspect. The feminine. And in that aspect, I am still alive. In that aspect, there was no so-called "alien" invasion.

Let me break it down for you.

I am still alive. Even though the fuselage of an airplane did fall from the sky and my physical body was crushed. The reason is that time, in its feminine aspect, operates inside what the academic-industrial complex would call quantum physics. But the quantum realm is simply the fundamental space of potential.

And here's why death is a liar.

Yes, I was playing chess in San Antonio park with Unc.(Three moves from checkmate, by the way). Yes, I saw a jet engine crash in the middle of Foothill Boulevard. Yes, it crushed a car. Yes, I heard a big boom over my head and everything went black.

In the masculine aspect, time is all mixed up in space. It is linear. Yes, in that version of time, so-called "aliens" attacked earth and caused all the planes to drop from the sky. In that version, yes, I was killed. But.

In the feminine aspect, the quantum realm, reality behaves differently, depending on if someone observes it. Instead of dead or alive, before or after, there is a third option. There is a version of reality that is still in a superposition, waiting to be observed. Waiting to be determined.

To conclude, the reason any of us can overcome death is because there is a version of us that does not die. Cannot. There is still a version of me that did finish that game and checkmate Unc. There is a version of me that dapped him up and went to pick my daughter up from school. There is a version where me and my daughter have fresh watermelon (with seeds) from the frutería, and we bring back a soft serve for Unc because that's what he asked for, and it's his business if he wants all that mucus and inflammation. There's a version where the three of us let the sun touch our skin and we close our eyes to enjoy it and all of our fingers are sticky with sugar.

That world exists if someone observes it. Just like this new world exists. This so-called afterlife.

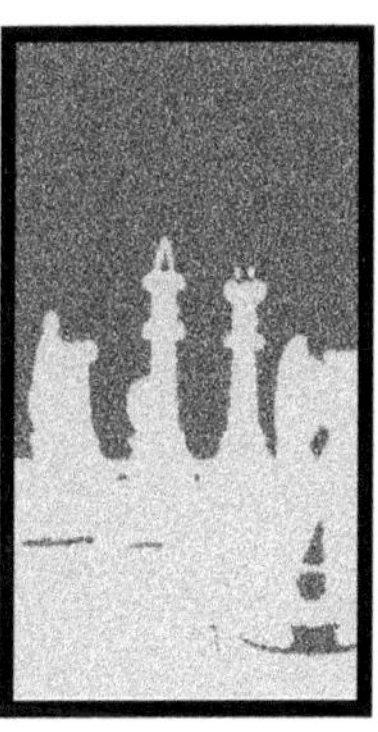

2 // Reggie Smith, New Orleans, LA

It was Super Sunday, and the second line was passing. I was re-watching Divorce in the Black because I love a good mess. Okay? My living room window faces the street, so I paused it. It's noisy, right? I'm hearing the horns, and the drums, and I look out and they got three bands, the queen, plus two DJs. I watched but I didn't go outside. It's been a while, but huh, I've seen the second line get shot up. Not I.

I stayed right inside with Tyler.

Especially since my nephew had just left. Him and that damn noise making dinosaur. I left that thing right in his bag. Talmbout 'uncle where Dino?'. Mommy didn't pack Dino. Cus' last time your lil stank butt stayed at my house, Dino going off all night, waking me up with some rawrghr. No Dino. You better eat your mac and cheese, and watch that tablet.

Anyway, I close the curtain. And I'm on my couch minding my Black business waiting for that second line to pass. Then the music stops. First the bands, then the DJ. I'm talmbout these folk qui-et. Black people not even that quiet at a funeral. Now that made me look outside.

The whole neighborhood out there just standing and watching while these egg-shaped things zoom down from the sky—vwoom—and come to a slow stop 'bout three inches from the ground. Falling into place one behind the other in a straight line down the street like a big zipper. Then somebody gonna say 'lemme go move my car'. Move my car? Man, if you don't move your ass.

And that's just what I did. Some big eggs come out of the sky — silently — and ya'll out there watching? I took myself right into that bunker. I'm one of the few buildings in the city with a sub-basement. And you know I'm on Youtube with my lil afro-survivalism channels. I was good for eight weeks. Water, food, power, comms, and yes I am a licensed gun owner. So I got the last of the snacks I like, start downloading a couple movies, and I'm going under that house.

Tell me why I'm on the first step to the base-ment (and these are concrete steps y'all) and I start to lose my footing. Laptop flying, snacks everywhere. And you know what I hear on my way down? Rawrghr.

My nephew really went in that bag and got out that dinosaur. And left it on my stairs! Y'all, the laptop hit the concrete before my head did. I had just bought that laptop. Y'all, I'm dead.

3 // Colonel S. Washington, Commander, 11th Air Defense Artillery Brigade, [Location Undisclosed]

At approximately sixteen hundred hours, we received reports of UAPs appearing in Russian and Chinese airspace. Quickly after that came reports from Europe, North Africa and South America. The US detected a large number in our own airspace. We were able to determine that it was not the act of a government or terrorist organization. At approximately sixteen fifteen, we received an audio message via SIPRnet with what we believed to be a synthesized voice communicating an aggressive posture. At that point, the UAPs dispersed toward critical assets, and fighter jets were scrambled to intercept.

As to my presence in this current location, I do not recall traveling here. I remember a loud boom at the command center and waking up shortly after at this locale. Currently awaiting further instruction.

4 // Mckenzie Gibson, Baltimore Maryland

I was going around the reservoir with Savannah when she takes out her earbud and says oh my god they just interrupted my podcast. I'm like aren't those pre-recorded, and she's like yes girl, but they interrupted it. I'm like that still doesn't make sense and she grabs me by the wrist and puts one of the earbuds in my hand. She has this look in her eyes like she just saw a dog get hit by a car. Stunned. Heartbroken.

I put in the earbud, and she pulls up TikTok and shows me a video of a mountain exploding. I asked where is that and she said Mt. Everest. It was NBC Nightly news. Lester Holt said it was unclear what the invaders wanted. They did however send what appeared to be an AI-generated audio message to all world governments. The content of that message, a single word: 'Observe.'

I'm thinking to myself Lester wouldn't lie. Then we heard a boom, and the reservoir started overflowing. We tried to run, but there was a lot of water. And I woke up in this place. Honestly not bad.

It kinda has a 1 Hotel Miami vibe.

Now let me find my friend. I know that girl Sav 'round here somewhere.

5 // Ronald Sharpe, Intelligence contractor, Fort Meade Maryland

If I was alive, I would be so cooked for telling you this, they would do me worse than Snowden. But since I'm not alive, I can tell you the first thing that happened is I got locked out of my terminal. I couldn't do anything but sit at my computer and watch. I saw a video showing someone clicking through different software. I didn't recognize them all, but it was definitely stuff like utilities, power grid, transportation, pretty much disabling them all. At the same time, I'm watching entire codebases deleted, servers wiped, data centers. If the whole internet was in the cloud, then the sky was falling. Everything, gone. Missile systems offlined. I watched all night as they dismantled everything, everywhere. There was no need of showing it in a video interface. I guess they wanted someone to see.

We talked about it in the Teams chat. Someone said it wasn't just data. They were digging to the undersea cables. Someone else said the aliens used an EMP to disable all the satellites in our orbit. They started crashing into each other, causing a Kessler effect — essentially a cascade of satellites crashing into satellites until there's so much debris floating in space that the planet is surrounded by it, making space travel impossible.

None of us knew what they wanted. All we had was the same line: 'Observe'. Eventually the internet dropped completely and I only had access to the local intranet. Then that down went with the power. The backup generators came on with the orange lights. I thought about just staying down there, 15 floors under. But what would I do when all the Aquafina and peanuts were gone? I looked around the room and realized I didn't like these people enough to ride out the apocalypse with them. So I got out of there. Other people made different decisions.

I kept my headphones on so it looked like I was going to the bathroom. While everyone was talking about what to do, I took the first elevator, then the hallway to the second elevator, skipped the lobby (probably too many people) and instead took the door in the cut that leads right to the courtyard. There was a lot of smoke and lights and gunfire. Artillery lit up big shapes in the sky that looked like clouds behind the clouds.

Next thing I hear is 'Stop or I will fire!'

And that was it. One of them Good Ol' Oorah boys got me. I recognized him, too. Security detail. He always had a certain vibe when he badged me in.

Guess he didn't recognize me. Maybe the headphones made me look like an alien.

6, 7 & 8 // Savannah St. Claire, Mckenzie Gibson, RA Khalil Earthborn

I was jogging at the Reservoir with my friend Mckenzie. I was listening to an old episode of The Read, and they interrupted it. The same message over and over.

Emergency. Seek shelter. Under attack. Source unknown. This is not a drill.

I didn't know they could interrupt a podcast.

"Savannah!"

Hey, boo!

"It's me Mckenzie."

I know who you are girl, you look the same.

"Oh, there's no mirrors in here."

Well, I can tell you, you look pretty good for a dead bitch.

"Bitch you look good."

"You are so much more than that sisters."

And who are you?

"I'm Khalil. Earthborn."

"Savannah, girl, anyway, is this like the Black heaven?"

There's a lot of us in here, huh?

"It's cosmic, the melanin. It was always deeper than skin."

"Sir, can we help you?"

He's lowkey kinda right, though. People did just start kicking it over here. Everybody asking the new person for the latest Tea on what happened on Earth with the attack. The stories got worse and worse the longer people lived. They took everything.

"You could only say they took everything from a human-centered point of view. The planet is still there, even if we aren't. Instead of saying they took everything from people, you could say they gave everything to The Earth."

"Okay, thank you, sir, we'll see you 'round."

I love you, Mac.

"I love you too, Sav. And girl, Khalil, uh, Earthborn?"

Girl.

9 // **Kyran Jackson, Los Angeles, CA**

In the years just after, there weren't many of us left. Global crop failure because of planetary cooling when they blew up the Himalayas. Everyone had to forage for food. I never enjoyed a blackberry so much in my life. I have a sweet tooth, and sweet things were hard to come by.

I used to want to be a comedian. Isn't that funny? I'd hang around lots, trying to pick up TV writing jobs. That's how I knew about the soundstage out by Kagel Canyon that cranked out movies that went straight to streaming. It was right by the San Fernando basin. And I knew there was groundwater. I figured that out one day on lunch while I was PAing a movie about a rural Georgia pastor who lives a double life as a pimp in Atlanta. I was out back smoking, and I noticed something you don't usually see in LA. A well.

When everything happened, I remembered the well. Water. I walked. There were fires, and the roads were cracked up. The aliens had gone; they did their work in about 30 hours. 30 hours that felt like weeks. So the only dangers were animals — and other people.

I lived by the well as long as I could, even though there was nothing else there but bramble and rocks. People would come and go. I didn't mind sharing. One family stayed for a month. A dad, with two boys.

Then a guy came one day, with this edgy energy. Like how dudes on coke at Jumbo's Clown Room used to be. I gave him some water, and we talked for a while. Mid-conversation he pulled a gun, and said start walking or die.

I thought about fighting, I could maybe take him. But I also didn't feel like killing him. And if I fought him, I would have to kill him. After everything I had seen by then, it just seemed pointless. So I walked.

Whatever humans had built, the aliens destroyed in one way or another. Timed explosions, lasers, force fields, booby traps. They did leave some simple things. I got lucky with the well.

I liked my walk. Los Angeles is beautiful

country. Whenever I spotted blackberries, I ate them. After a while, I was coming out of the canyon, and couldn't believe what I was seeing. The corner of a building still standing. White brick. I walked around to check it out, and something else I couldn't believe. A refrigerator case. It must have been some kind of convenience store. I moved the weeds that were grown around it, and it was full! No power of course, but still. Gatorade, Coke, Dasani, Monster you name it. That stuff doesn't go bad. Let him keep the well, shit.

I obviously didn't want the Dasani because I had plenty of water already. But I wanted to start slow, so I decided on a Gatorade. The blue one because it tastes the coldest. I grabbed the handle, and I'm thinking about how much I've been missing something sweet. The blackberries were getting me by, but this was a dream.

I opened the refrigerator case, and felt the worst heat I've ever felt. I saw a flash of flames, and heard the boom. That was it.

I understood the alien mission. If people built it, they destroyed it. But rigging a soda case with explosives? That just seems spiteful. Something a human would do. Someone who wanted to keep the sugar all to themselves.

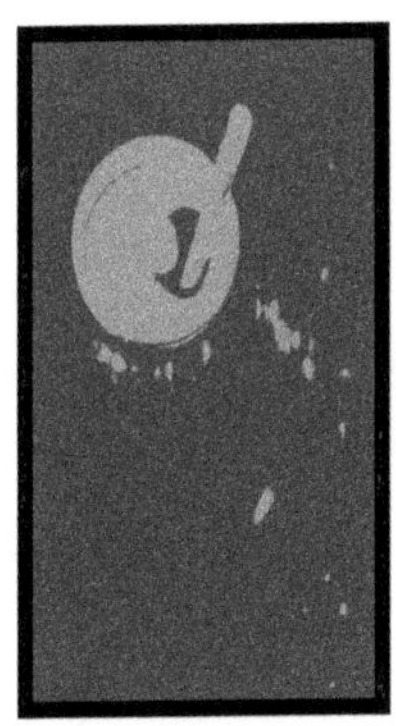

10 // James Carter, New Jersey

The day it happened was my grandson's birthday. He had just gotten tall enough to ride El Toro alone. So we drove up to Six Flags for the day. We got to the park, and he went straight to the roller coaster. I got us both fast passes even though I didn't ride anything. He went again, and again and again. Eventually I said it's time for lunch, and he begged me for one more ride. So I let him. It was his birthday.

I got myself a Cherry Coke slush while he was in line, and I drank it while his car climbed slowly to the top. He waved at me just before the first drop. Then boom. An explosion that burned my skin and melted my sunglasses. I think if it wasn't for the sunglasses I would have been partially blind.

I made it out of the park in a haze of smoke, and I walked around for I don't know how long just waving at my grandson. Things got pretty violent while there were still guns, and I had one pointed at me more than once.

But I guess they figured what's the point of

killing a crazy old man with nothing.

Things changed after all the guns were gone. Well, it was really the bullets that ran out. And then the guns were useless. There were fewer people then, too. We were all so tired, not just from the aliens but from life before. The craziness.

Eventually, seeing another person was so rare, you wouldn't think of hurting them. It was just a strange idea. All of us were starved that way. I was ashamed I hadn't always thought of other people like that. Rare, sacred.

In the last year I was alive, I came across this village. I guess you could call it that. A few families living in shacks made of corrugated steel and wood scraps.

I was old and dirty, but they welcomed me. Sometimes the people got together and told stories about what happened. Most of us believed it was a reset. Maybe even Earth herself called in some reinforcements. People said that.

One of the women there was an engineer.

She built a few windmills powerful enough to light the place.

The youngest kids there had never seen the world the way it was before. The lights coming on every night was like magic for them, and they would play in the bright spot in the middle of the shacks.

I fell asleep one night listening to them play. Then I woke up here.

Best sleep of my life.

***

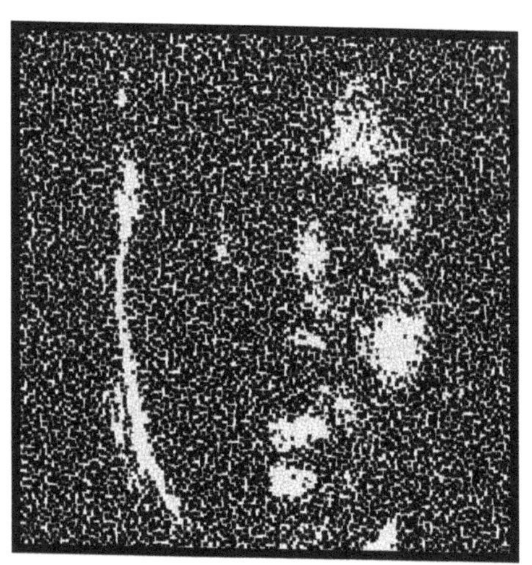

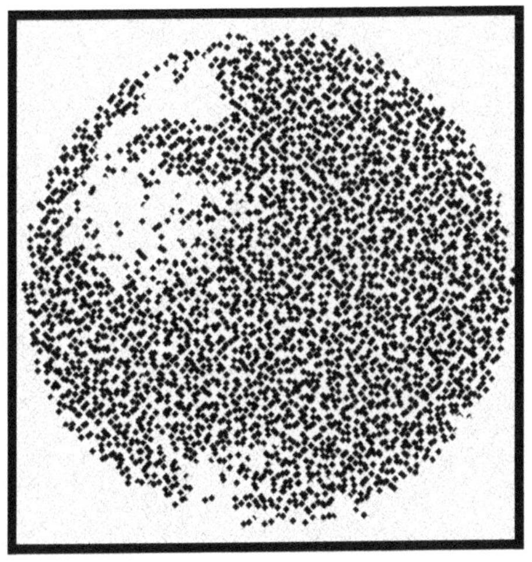

ABOUT THE AUTHOR

Evan Ross Burton is a poet and fiction writer whose work has appeared in various journals, live performances, and anthologies.

He is a Cave Canem fellow and an advertising copywriter. Evan lives in Baltimore, Maryland.

Everyday Black People in Strange Situations is his first collection of short stories.

To learn more, visit:

hotsecondbooks.com
heyevan.com

***